MW01173259

Bellflower

A novel-in moments

Mary Pensel White

ISBN 979-8-9878309-4-9 (paperback)

ISBN 979-8-9878309-5-6 (ebook)

Published by Type Eighteen Books

www.typeeighteenbooks.com

For my mother, Carol Jean Vensel,
who loved me, and loved books

"There are only two or three human stories, and they go on repeating themselves as fiercely as if they had never happened before."

—Willa Cather

Author Note

Life is lived in moments. Memories don't follow a strict chronology. I'd like to think that when our days draw to a close, we remember the people and events of our lives in a series of fragments and flashes: beautiful, brief images creating an impressionistic whole of the person we were, our own unique story painted in vivid miniatures.

The sections and chapters of this novel can be read in any order. Each third chapter follows the moments and stories of one family. If you'd like to read more about the Hanleys after Chapter One, then skip to Chapter Four, then Seven, and so on. Some sections in this book are many pages long; some are very brief, maybe a couple of paragraphs. If you're short on time, dip into a short section, anywhere in the book. If you have a free afternoon, choose one of the longer parts. There is no strict chronology here either, no reason you can't do whatever you feel like doing. Start from the end! Pick a random page! Really, this book is your oyster. In the end, it all amounts to the same thing—a telling of the moments from the lives of these characters. The building of the story is up to you.

Contents

CHAPTER 19 HANLEY

CHAPTER 20 MOORE

CHAPTER 21 HALLOWICZ

Chapter

1

Hanley

Boy Meets Girl

The party theme was the Roaring Twenties, although none of them had been born then. Glittering headbands and fringed skirts were rented from a costume supplier the women had emailed each other about in the preceding weeks. Some ladies wore bobbed wigs, the bangs severe across their foreheads. Punctuating the sequins and feathers, the satin and silk, were the men in suits, mostly their own but with minor, festive flourishes added.

Glen Hanley sat on a leather barstool at the newly installed wet bar, thinking how strange it was to celebrate someone's fiftieth birthday by embracing a distant decade, to adopt an era that had nothing to do with any of them and have a party in someone's garage, no matter how expertly finished it was.

Glen Hanley was a tall man but from a distance, he had a hunched, small look. A dark shock of hair combed over a broad head, wide shoulders, and a stomach flatter than most men his age. In good working order, he felt, an attractive specimen if the reactions from many female customers at the bank were any indication.

He ordered a scotch and soda from his wife's PTA friend and hostess of the party, Susan Gleeson. She twisted the cap, and a spray of club soda vapors dotted her face. They both smiled. He had met her several years before, returning from work to find four women huddled over a mound of papers at his kitchen table, had listened politely through the introductions and explanations about the upcoming school fundraiser, all the while wondering what was to be done about his dinner. Both daughters were busy with afterschool activities then, and his wife Janet had given up the custom of regular dinners. But nothing had changed for him. He still worked at the bank, still played in his tennis group on Tuesdays and Thursdays. He, Glen Hanley, still wanted dinner.

Susan Gleeson slid a sweaty glass across the bar. Her eyes glittered underneath a fringe of dark hair. It was July and—despite the central air conditioning vented in from the house—hot. Glen Hanley squinted, trying to remember the color of Susan's actual hair under the wig.

She leaned over the bar, her bosom two mounds of dough, reflected in duplicate on the polished surface. "I like your suit," she breathed into his ear.

Glen Hanley looked down at the pinstripes and white tie, rented, imagining his wife had set him up for ridicule.

"You look dangerous," Susan Gleeson added.

In the center of the ceiling, a disco ball had been hung under the garage door opener. Late summer, late evening, the sun spilling orange across the meager street. Flecks of colored light radiated weakly from the glass fixture, which turned and turned from its omniscient position, some tacky imitation of the earth. Later, when the recycling bin brimmed with bottles and the brie began to harden and ooze, the disco ball reached its full glory. By then, the overhead lights had been dimmed, and the dance floor became crowded.

Once again, Glen Hanley was sitting on the barstool, chastened by his wife's wisecrack about the banality of mortgage lending and both numbed and incited enough by his fifth scotch and soda to leave her dancing alone to "Night Moves," which had nothing to do with the 1920s either. And once again, Susan Gleeson appeared with her cleavage above red satin. Susan Gleeson with her refreshing beverages. How unbelievably lucky Doug Gleeson was, he thought, to have a finished garage and a terrific fiftieth birthday party when he, Glen Hanley, couldn't even get a hot dinner most nights.

So when the next song on the Gleesons's playlist was "Blinded By the Light," a song he had blared in his childhood bedroom on Santa Marina Street, his mother coughing under an afghan on the living room couch and his twin sisters laughing or fighting nearby (because Glen Hanley had been surrounded by women his entire life), when this song started, making him feel nineteen years old and not fifty himself in seven months, the rhythmic drumbeat, the expressive guitar like a lone, pleading voice, the electronic sounds altering the insulated garage into something as foreign as a moonscape, Glen grabbed Susan's hand, pulled her around the bar (his own wife be damned), and brought her to the newly laid dance floor.

Death Comes for Man

Kizzy Hanley parked her car near the fire hydrant where one summer, her sister Lurie slipped in a puddle and got a concussion. Their mother blamed Kizzy, who was older and therefore, in charge. The hydrant had been leaking for several days and the neighborhood kids had sworn a pact of silence, filling cups and bowls for their own purposes, dipping their heads under the faint stream. Lurie, excitable and absentminded, seemed destined for accidents. Even now, Kizzy had a text that Lurie's flight from Denver was snow-delayed. They'd spend the evening worrying and checking the airline's website, thinking and talking about Lurie.

Slowly, Kizzy retrieved her purse and the take-out bag from the passenger seat. She'd been staying at her parents' house (her *mother's* house she'd have to get used to saying) for three nights. Ever since her father collapsed at his Thursday tennis game. There was no reason for it, no sense to be made. He is, *was,* fifty-six years old. Kizzy bit her lip, shook the wave off.

Her mother was where she'd left her, cleaning the refrigerator. Her backside in the blue polyester pants protruded from the open freezer door, jiggling as she scrubbed. Boxes of vegetables, cellophane-wrapped meat, an ice-covered Ben & Jerry's, all of it on the marble countertop, all of it in individualized tiny puddles.

"Almost finished then, Mom?" Kizzy asked. "The food is melting."

Her head came out, face shiny from the cold, eyes glassy. "What?"

Kizzy helped her load the things back in then gathered plates, forks, and napkins and took it all to the kitchen barstools. They hadn't eaten in the dining room since she'd arrived. Already they were starting new ways of being.

"You don't have to stay," her mother said for the tenth time. "I know you've got your job, your apartment."

"Mom, it's three miles away. Everything will stay the same there."

Her apartment. Draped over the chair in her bedroom, the colorful Japanese gown (no one to see it), the toiletries in a straight line across the marble vanity. The quiet and the dark.

She dished Kung Pao chicken for her mother. "I'll stay with you through the service. I want to see Lurie." Lurie's expanding figure, Lurie with her happy marriage and little miracle on the way.

Her mother nodded. "All right then, Kizzy."

The clock in the hallway chimed six o'clock. An heirloom of sorts, given by Kizzy's grandmother when her daughter married Glen Hanley, it rang every half hour. Can't you change the settings, her father would ask. But Janet Hanley insisted she didn't notice at all, having lived with it for so long.

During the chiming, Kizzy and her mother looked at each other. A brief moment, nothing to say. Marvelous and terrifying, Kizzy thought, how quickly we go, how long we stay.

Girl Grows Up

Janet sat on the edge of her bed, a suitcase open beside her. The list was written on a sheet of notebook paper, ragged at the edge where she had ripped it from an old book of math notes. There were three entries, and she'd been trying for most of the afternoon to think of more.

Important things that happened to me recently:

1. Lost my job at Iron Works.

2. Slept with Ricky a few times.

3. Colored my hair blonde.

Seeing the achievements of the past year listed in this way made her even more determined. Losing the job had been a relief. She couldn't imagine the exciting events of her future life having anything at all to do with welding. As to the second item, Ricky was just a friend, one whose company she could tolerate after several drinks. The blonde hair was the only entry with promise. Already, she felt more noticeable.

She rifled through the items in the suitcase, looking again for her favorite dress, worn once to her uncle's wedding. Blue with swirls of white, a captured sky.

Barstow was a sleepy town, a crossroads soldiering on in the shadow of its mining days. First silver in nearby Calico, then borax until there wasn't any more. The town was proud of its position at the end of Route 66—"the transportation hub of the western Mojave"—but it was difficult to imagine the bustle of immigrants when all Janet could envision were ways to get out.

Their three-bedroom ranch house was home to eleven: Janet, her parents, six siblings, her aunt and a cousin. They shared one bathroom and the square of grass in the back. Her father was a mid-level welder at Iron Works and her mother took occasional jobs babysitting or cleaning houses. Her father hadn't spoken to Janet since she'd been fired from the front office.

The door squeaked open, and her sister Bea came in. Bea's eyes widened when she saw the suitcase, and she spun around and left. Like the shifting air before a storm, the family had sensed Janet's intentions.

A faint knock sounded at the door.

"Janet?" It was her mother, a slight courtesy before opening the door anyway. She entered, wringing her hands on a dish towel. "That's your brother's suitcase," she said.

Janet's brother, Shawn, had recently moved to San Diego for a construction job but returned after four months. He lived at his girlfriend's house because their father had kicked him out.

"He's not using it," Janet said. She wanted to add: And he never will. None of you will. We're on the Titanic, watching the frigid water as one by one, we're pulled under.

Her mother wrapped the towel around her fist. "He might," she said.

Janet looked at her then, this woman who'd had seven children by the age of twenty-seven, before having her uterus removed after a stage three cancer. These, the only important facts of her mother's life, often recited to other women for witnessing. Everyone said Janet was her spitting image, but Janet didn't see it.

"Where you going?" her mother asked, with something like hope or envy in her voice.

"LA," Janet said. "Lauren said I could rent the extra room in her apartment."

"Lauren from Waverly?"

She nodded. Waverly Elementary, a million years ago.

"She's a nice girl?" her mother asked.

Janet stood up and closed the suitcase. "I'll find a job," she said. "I'll send you some money for the Toyota."

Her mother raised her hand, blocking a portion of her face.

"I owe Daddy four hundred still," Janet insisted. "I'll pay it."

Her mother stared a moment more, then flung the dish towel over her shoulder and left.

Janet walked through the house, past her sisters sprawled in front of the television, past her cousin who sat on the porch, staring down the dirty street.

And her mother never came out to watch her leave.

After two years in Los Angeles, Janet made another list. Among the occurrences documented: a job at a dingy coffee shop, night classes in history and art, a bitter fight with a roommate, three days of debauchery in Tijuana, a visit from her brother, an argument with the same brother during that visit, a new television with a built-in VCR, a protracted relationship with an aspiring singer, more night classes, a trek home when her grandmother died, a Bob Seger concert at the Forum, a broken wrist while rollerblading, a brief, emotionless liaison, a sailboat ride in Long Beach, a job at a grocery store, and a trip to San Francisco where she fell in love and subsequently, settled down.

CHAPTER

Moore

Couple Starts a Family

Terri Moore finds an empty chair in The Quiet Room, amidst the plush pillows and chenille throws. She puts her feet up on an ottoman, one of several beige islands on the sea of blue carpet. It feels wonderful under her feet. Her eight-hour shift has just ended—three facials, two waxes, and a laser treatment for rosacea. She wears flat, expandable shoes, having learned this lesson over the eight years she's been working at Spa Energe. Still, the soles of her feet ache, merely from the standing. From the leaning, a familiar tightening in the muscles of her lower back.

"That you, Terri baby?" Valerio, a new masseuse in his early twenties, glides into the room.

She puts a wrist behind her head and leans back. "Just resting for a minute," she says.

"You go, girl." Valerio claps twice and disappears into Room Seven, where he has a four o'clock Pure Relaxation Session.

Terri, eyes upward, notices the gold tone of the ceiling. Wall sconces of brushed bronze emit a soft yellow and across the room, a portrait of water is flecked with incandescent paint. The whole room shimmers. It's the third remodel since Terri began working here, after completing the esthetician program at Cardiff College. After the unexpected divorce at age thirty-four. The public's idea of what escape looks like is always evolving, she's discovered.

From the cubby near the front desk, she gathers her silver purse and black sweater. She arrived at nine that morning in the characteristic overcast grayness, the morning dullness never shown in television programs about southern California, about the beach towns. Now, outside is more like what they do show—blue skies, lush leaves, the sun white as a spotlight.

She finds her car, a Lexus sedan she can only afford on a lease. Two quick turns and she's heading north on Pacific Coast Highway. She still has the three-bedroom, ranch-style home in Huntington Beach, the first and only house she's ever owned. Randy loved its proximity to the ocean; at forty-six, his body is still lean and brown from surfing. The house has beige stucco in front, a modest yard with citrus trees in the back. Perfect for kids, Randy had said. Karly was born first, shortly after Terri's twenty-fourth birthday, and Tyler arrived fourteen months later. How in the world did *that* happen, people would ask with a gleam in their eye, an unspoken judgement. In the early years, she and Randy couldn't keep their hands off each other. But they learned to be more careful. Two babies will teach you that.

Terri turns into the short driveway and parks behind Tyler's white hatchback. He's home early from his job at the country club, where he drives an armored car that sweeps golf balls from the pocked grass of the driving range. A part-time job for spending money, while he finishes his first year at Cal State Long Beach. Karly's a student at Long Beach, too, in pediatric nursing. Terri often wonders how her dramatic daughter will handle a screaming child, because it was Karly who always ran a high fever, Karly who was dunked into lukewarm baths in the middle of the night or rushed to the emergency room for ear infections and fast-spreading rashes. Always in the darkest, deepest part of night, her shrieks slicing through the house. Randy took charge in these situations, calming Terri and Karly both, giving directions. When he finally moved out, the kids were past the wailing stage.

The curtains are drawn when Terri walks in. The sun reaches through one small opening and becomes a wedge of swirling air. In a few moments, her eyes adjust. She has almost reached the kitchen when she notices Tyler on the couch.

"Mom."

Something about his voice, something about the darkness, raises the hair on her neck. "What is it?" she asks.

He stands up, this six-foot-tall boy, this nineteen-year-old with the same green eyes and the scar from a sharp tree branch over his left eyebrow, still L-shaped but its edges blurred now. Both of her children are like gigantic, warped versions of themselves; she sometimes feels disoriented in their presence.

Tyler holds out a piece of paper, an envelope.

Terri takes it and quickly reads the letter inside. She looks at her son, who avoids her gaze, then reads the paper again. "Paternity?" she asks.

"Remember when I went to Fullerton with Simon?"

A rumbling in her ears. She shakes her head.

"Last year," he says. "Almost a year ago, I guess."

"You guess?"

Arms crossed over his chest. "I met a girl at a party. Amber."

Terri finds the name on the document, under the State of California seal.

Tears in his green eyes, a helplessness.

And she feels the perfect day clamoring outside, the sunshine pressing against the stucco walls of the house, squeezing the life from her.

Tyler runs his hands through his hair. "I don't even know her, Mom."

Boy Meets Girl

"Put a couple of balloons on the tree outside," Amber says. "There's string in the kitchen, top drawer by the oven."

A sliding sound, items shifted.

"Got it?" she calls.

"Yeah."

Her brother, in a sullen mood, dropped off early at her apartment so he wouldn't be at their parents' house alone. William is fifteen and on the outs with their mother, who had errands to run before the party.

Joy ambles down the hall in her party dress, white with yellow needlepoint sunrays. "Mommy, what time is it?"

Amber turns from the table, where she has arranged a stack of pink plates next to Joy's chosen party favors: fake jeweled necklaces for the girls, Matchbox cars for the boys. She is six years old today and already has unshakable ideas about gender. Amber herself was a tomboy growing up. Her older sister preferred dresses and dolls, but Amber spent her days with scabbed knees and tangled hair, dirt under her nails.

"Twenty more minutes and they'll come," she tells her daughter.

Joy runs to the door. "Uncle William! The balloons look awesome!"

Even Amber's sullen brother has to grin at this. He comes back into the house, pulled along by Joy, who begins a discourse on the habits of hippopotami inspired by a recent trip to the zoo.

Amber takes a moment, looks around. They've been in this apartment for eight months. Joy has celebrated every other birthday at her grandparents' house, while Amber finished college and started a job, saved money for a car and furniture, then for the security deposit and first and last month's rent. Two bedrooms, the kitchen window overlooking a grassy area where Joy keeps a pink wooden bench her grandfather built. It was never easy, still isn't easy, and Amber is keenly aware of the debt she owes her parents.

An hour later, the party is in full swing. Four boys and four girls from Joy's first grade class are happily blowing bubbles onto the grass. Amber looks out from the kitchen, where she is washing chocolate frosting from somebody's sneaker. A car door slams, then Tyler walks down the sidewalk.

Her breath catches. She can already imagine her conversation with Lurie, her best friend. *He hasn't grown up*, Lurie will say. *Don't set yourself up for disappointment.* Lurie had an abortion the year before but stayed with her boyfriend, Brandon, who was loyal and kind and partially heartbroken afterwards. They argue about other things now instead of talking about it. Amber isn't sure if they'll stay together.

On the sidewalk, Joy drops her plastic jar of bubbles then picks it up. She looks toward the apartment. Amber makes it to the door as Joy says "Hi, Daddy" and hugs Tyler. Her tone is casual, but Amber sees the restraint, the hope. It makes the back of her throat clench.

There have been other parties, other events. Tyler shows up, usually. Sometimes he brings his mother, whom Amber has learned to trust over the years. If it wasn't for Terri, she would have fought the custody agreement, which allows Tyler to take Joy for two weekends a month. The unofficial provision is that Terri always be present. Tyler was eighteen when Joy was born. Amber was just twenty-three but forced to be the mature one.

On Joy's second birthday, Tyler overslept and missed the clown Amber had hired. On her third birthday, he showed up with a six-pack of Budweiser for an afternoon picnic and drank all of it. Once he pushed Joy too high on a swing, and she fell off and sprained her wrist. At times, he came through. The "Spring Sing" at Joy's preschool, when he brought a bunch of petite yellow carnations. The three hours he stood in line for the Finding Nemo ride at Disneyland.

"Hi, sweetie," he says now to his daughter, and something in his voice makes Amber look up. He is different, his face more formed, the line of his jaw defined and speckled with golden hair that sparks in the sun.

Favors packed up, eight first-graders loaded into minivans and SUVs. Bits of paper collected from the grass, smeared pink plates stacked in the trash can. For once, Tyler stays and helps.

"You don't have to," Amber tells him.

"It's okay," he says.

Amber's mother waits around until she can't wait anymore. She shoots meaningful glances at Amber. "I guess we'll get going," she finally says.

"Thanks for your help, Mom." Amber hugs her and punches William's shoulder lightly, which brings a scowl. She leaves Joy in her bedroom, sitting on the floor surrounded by her new toys. The center of everything.

Tyler hovers in the kitchen. His tall frame seems out of place, and she has to walk around him, a huge obstacle, to continue putting dishes into the dishwasher.

"It was nice talking to you the other day," he says.

She faces him, remembering the conversation about Joy's party, about other things.

"There's something different with you," he says. "Your hair."

She reaches up. "Highlights," she says, her face warming.

"I like it." He puts his hands into the pockets of his plaid shorts. "I'm changing jobs."

"I thought you liked fixing computers?"

He smiles, and she turns away and keeps busy at the sink. "Information technology," he says. "They gave me a promotion."

She moves dishes, turns on the faucet. "That's great!"

"The support stays the same," he says.

"I know." She looks out the window at the pink bench, gleaming in the sunlight. "I was just happy for you."

"I'm sorry," he says. "I never know what I mean to say when I'm around you."

"So it's my fault?"

"No, hey, turn around. Listen."

She turns, and he has crossed the room, stands before her. He is so close she can't see beyond him.

He blinks rapidly. "I feel like I've known you forever, Amber, or I don't know you at all. Sometimes, I wonder what you're doing."

"You can always call us," she says.

"I think about seeing you, about—"

She turns away, impatient. So selfish, she thinks. All about him. "Do you want to take Joy more?" she asks. "Because I think that's a good idea." She dries her hands with a paper towel. "She loves you but when she hasn't seen you for a while, I think it's confusing. Her feelings and what to do with them. Do you know what I mean?"

And Tyler steps forward, turns her again, and grabs her wrists. He pulls her hands onto his chest. She feels the hard muscle there, the warmth and the swell of his breath. He smells like an open field. He is the boy in the bedroom at the party, all smoky air and throbbing base from the stereo in the living room. He is the hint of green in Joy's wide eyes. He is something new, a broad forehead with the faintest of lines, a determined grasp, intent.

"Yes," he says. "Yes, I do."

CHAPTER

3

Hallowicz

Woman Suffers Loss of Loved One

"Goddamn, disgusting pigs." Mrs. Hallowicz bent to retrieve an empty beer bottle from where it was wedged between two stripped fence posts. Clutching the glass until her knuckles turned white, she peered through the gaping hole at the Gleesons' house.

"No time to mow the lawn," she said, straightening up. "Grass knee high, porch chairs covered in soot." She walked over to a garbage container, partially hidden behind an old sycamore. "Workmen here for three weeks, pounding, yelling in Spanish, running that goddamn saw all hours and for what?"

Three houses down from Mrs. Hallowicz's, a silver car paused at a driveway then continued down the quiet street. This event caused a momentary pause in Mrs. Hallowicz's diatribe. Curiosity always trumped complaining, the latter she had ample opportunity for, the former piqued very infrequently.

Her gravelly voice picked up where she'd left off. "Says they're working on the garage. For their kids when they visit. For retirement. Make the kids do the yard work, I say!"

The bottle made a loud thump at the bottom of the trash can, giving Mrs. Hallowicz a meager sense of satisfaction.

She turned and walked toward the backyard, her rain galoshes stirring dirt down the narrow walkway framed by fence and house. She reached out and touched the rough wall now and then.

"Those women with their shrill voices, baseballs over my fence for years, kids yelling, and now, music until two o'clock in the morning! Goddamn Gleesons."

One corner of the yard was enclosed with chicken coop wire, a project completed years before. My son is fifty-three years old, Mrs. Hallowicz thought, the realization coming as a familiar shock. Robbie. Robert. Rob. Over the years, his name changing as his body grew. Robbie for the lanky boy, all elbows and knees, rolling his little metal cars around the house. Robert for the young cadet, the shadow-eyed veteran, the tired father of twins. Rob in typical middle age—paunch, slumped shoulders, wounded eyes. Who moves to New Mexico, Mrs. Hallowicz wanted to know, and over the years, she hadn't found an adequate answer to the question.

The wire was rust-marked but stable. She remembered her husband and Robbie working on the cage one autumn afternoon, the yard a confluence of colored leaves around their feet. Wilson leaning over, talking to the boy. Robbie peering up, the hammer extended from his hand, as long as his slender calf. Mrs. Hallowicz had watched from the window, work to do in the kitchen. She wished now she had come outside, had kicked through the colorful piles to hear what they were saying.

She reached into her apron pocket and pulled out a sheath of cool lettuce leaves. Lowering herself down to her knees, she folded the leaves in half and pushed them through an opening in the wire. Against the wooden fence, she settled into herself.

In time, a grayish snout appeared, followed by a long, wrinkled neck. Finally, the shining eyes, murky but wide.

"Hello, you old thing," Mrs. Hallowicz said.

The turtle was faded and monotone, the color of dirt. His shell was a perfect study in symmetry: a series of rounded squares, textured and ridged, the outline pinched like the crust of a pie. Reptilian, birdlike, his feet were narrow and clawed. She hadn't picked him up in years but when she did, his legs would move slowly, bicycling, as though he couldn't distinguish air from land. She remembered the bottom of his shell to be soft and whitish.

He meandered towards the lettuce, which had fallen into a bare, grass-free corner of the pen. Then, inexplicably, he stopped. His patience was one of the things she appreciated most about him. Extending his wrinkly neck, the skin so similar to her own now, he turned his head from side to side, listening. Or smelling. She couldn't be sure. She only knew, after years of watching him, that he was very, very smart.

"What is it?" she asked, craning her own neck towards the Gleesons's. "Did that racket keep you up?"

The turtle lifted his snout then retracted a bit into his shell.

"I know," she said, her voice lowered. "I know."

She lingered by the pen, listening to the distant voices of her neighbors, watching the turtle as he remained motionless and then, after some time, continued his slow trek towards the lettuce. Finally, he lowered his gray head but did not eat.

"Be a good boy, Gordon."

Robbie named him Flash Gordon, after the comic book character. It was a joke at first, because Flash Gordon's special power was speed and of course, turtles are slow. But not long after Wilson brought the turtle home, Robbie swore he saw it move very quickly, startled by a car backfiring. For many years, he tried to duplicate this reaction, by sneaking up on the turtle, by throwing rocks into the pen from a distance, by leading the neighbors' dogs and cats to the cage.

"Stop tormenting that turtle," Mrs. Hallowicz would yell from the kitchen window. Secretly, she found her son's efforts a little amusing, but now that she was old and slow herself, the memories brought shame. Things shouldn't be forced to go against their nature. Eventually, she dropped the Flash from his name, and he became just Gordon.

She trudged back to the front of the house, trailing her hand along the outer wall, her feet following the groove in the land. As she stepped around the corner, a shadow slapped onto the driveway.

"Mrs. Hallowicz?"

She looked up and there stood Sandy Gleeson, the neighbors' youngest, moved away years ago. A memory flashed: Sandy, six years old, falling on the gravel out front, crying squeaky cries, reaching her arms up as Mrs. Hallowicz approached.

Sandy was a grown woman now, dressed in jeans and a white, button-up shirt. Man's clothes, Mrs. Hallowicz thought. She continued towards her porch.

"Do you remember me, Mrs. Hallowicz? It's Sandy Gleeson. I used to help you with your flowers?"

The old woman's eyes pinched as she faced her. "Yes, I remember. I'm old but not senile."

The younger woman smiled. Her teeth were brilliant white. "I'm visiting my parents. It's almost noon, and they're still sleeping." She chuckled. "Must have been some party."

"It was very loud and very late," Mrs. Hallowicz said.

"I hope it didn't disturb you?"

She shrugged. "I'm tired."

Sandy smiled again. It seemed to be her most natural expression. "I wanted to say hello and see if there's anything you need?"

Mrs. Hallowicz felt a warmth on her face. "Of course not," she snapped. Her shoulders rose almost to her ears. "I need your parents to keep their trash off my lawn."

The words sprayed and settled like shards of glass.

Sandy looked over her shoulder towards the house. "I should check on them." She took a few steps but turned back. Her eyes were bright, the whites reflected against the white of her shirt and the smooth strands of white clouds behind her. "You take care of yourself, Mrs. Hallowicz. You know, I always think of you when I see flowers."

Mrs. Hallowicz waved her hand violently. "Goodbye." With some force, she pulled her front door open. Inside, the house was dark. She stood in the foyer, breathing, and reached up to wipe some water from her cheek. "Goddamn," she said.

Wilson brought the turtle home from the roofing company when they settled in Bellflower and bought the simple, three-bedroom house with the unattached garage. She had grown up in Milwaukee, before her family came west during her junior year of high school. When Wilson showed her the house, it reminded her of the houses from her childhood. Simple, modest, lined up orderly along the street, no one structure begging more attention than the next.

Mrs. Hallowicz ran one of her late husband's handkerchiefs under the kitchen faucet, squeezed out the excess water and sat down in her recliner. She put the cloth on her forehead.

She met Wilson at a school dance then again during the summer after graduation, while he apprenticed to become a roofer and Mrs. Hallowicz (who was Betsy Springer then) filled out college applications and never mailed them, helped her mother around the house, and drank whiskey sours with her girlfriends at the school after hours.

Robbie was born nine months and three weeks after their wedding. Mrs. Hallowicz viewed this as some kind of divine intervention rather than youthful misunderstanding because she had, in most ways, always been a good girl. She believed herself to be pregnant when she and Wilson stood on the steps of City Hall, and she believed it now.

Wilson had a coworker who had recently purchased a new house, and his basset hound wouldn't stop digging near a boulder in the back yard. That's how he found the turtle. He had no idea how old it was or how long it had lived there. He brought it to work to see if anyone would take it.

Mrs. Hallowicz sat up in the recliner, remembering Robbie's excited expression when he looked inside the box. The innocence, the wonder.

She removed the cool handkerchief from her forehead. She was prone to headaches. They'd start above her ears, a general tightening, spread over her eyes, recede along her scalp. It made her think of savages and shrunken heads, as though her body was drying and shrinking. Slowly, her eyes focused on the darkened living room, the sheen of light through the dusty curtains. She heard a distant lawnmower.

It's Sunday, she remembered. Robbie in dress pants, never long enough to keep up with his growth, sneakers to church because his loafers were too small again. At his peak, Robert was six feet tall, but now he was shrinking, too. On Thanksgiving two years ago, he was a faded, smaller version of what she had remembered.

Outside, a steady plunking sound. Mrs. Hallowicz's head popped up, craned around the side of the recliner.

Plunk. Plunk. Plunk.

Laughter and a banging. Plunk, plunk, plunk.

She pushed her hands against the armrests and pushed herself up. She passed a photograph of Robert in his pressed uniform with its colorful pins, the hat stiff and crown-like.

Plunk. Plunk. Someone was playing ping-pong.

"Goddamn Gleesons," she said. "Can't I have any peace?"

She opened the door and trudged down the front steps, over the path, and through the threshold to the Gleeson's sidewalk. It used to be gravel, and she remembered the day they moved in, the two boys and the little girl, a mop of reddish-blonde hair and round knees. The screaming, the laughing, the life.

Mrs. Hallowicz stopped and looked. The Gleesons's garage door was open and from the center of the room, something threw sparks of colored light into the bright afternoon. Red, purple, blue and diamond white. Underneath, two figures on each side of a green expanse.

Plunk, plunk, plunk.

Her eyes were watering again, and something made her turn and look towards Gordon's pen, her view obstructed by the fence dividing her house from the neighbors'. She felt a pull now and hurried back the way she came. Along the sidewalk, down the path, across her thinning yard. And when the sparks had left her eyes and she could see, there was the shell, immobile, the bumpy legs splayed alongside it, twitching above the scarred earth. Gordon never lingered in the center of the pen like that. He liked privacy and quiet as she did. His head was bent strangely, she noticed.

Mrs. Hallowicz's eyes followed the ragged line of the fence, porous wood and rusted nails, which seemed to extend past the horizon itself. She pressed her fist to her mouth and leaned heavily against the house, which was still stable enough to hold her up although its stucco poked her in a thousand places.

CHAPTER

4

Hanley

A Childhood Adventure

She thought of mimes, with their white faces and startled eyes, the way they press outward and upward as though in a box. That's what her heart felt like, trapped, thumping against her ribcage over and over again.

Here, next to the tall, endless fence, the grass was warm and prickly under her bare feet. She leaned against the wood, and the head of a nail caught for a moment on her t-shirt. She shifted to release the fabric. Crouching, waiting, she felt safe.

"Crap!"

A startled voice, probably Billy Baird. The smallest of their group and usually found first.

Footsteps slapped against the sidewalk; there were whispers she couldn't make out. She may have heard her name.

This was the part she liked. Waiting for the discovery, the hairs on her arms standing straight up, excitement like fingers on her neck. Her older sister Kizzy could barely stand hiding. She'd rather be "it." And when she found someone, Kizzy roughly yanked them by the shirt or hair, always bragging and teasing. When Kizzy was forced to hide, she'd find an obvious place or purposely cough or make noise until they found her. Then she'd pretend to be disappointed.

"Lurie!"

Now she really did hear her name. Pressing her shoulders against the fence, she turned in her crouched position, trying to find a crack to look through.

"Come on, Lurie. You're last."

It was Kizzy's voice, and she sounded irritated that her little sister had won again.

"No going into other yards!" This voice belonged to Mack, older brother to Billy, one year older than Lurie but always acting like he was much more. The brothers had lived on their street since she could remember. During the long, hot summer days, the boys would wander outside after breakfast and wait to see who'd show up. Sara Lomero, the fifth of their neighborhood group, was away at a Girl Scout camp that week. She'd missed all the fun with the broken fire hydrant. They'd kept it from their parents and were secretly building a moat behind the Simpkins's house. Mr. and Mrs. Simpkins worked all day, and their kids were grown, so no one was ever home. They'd dug a narrow groove and had been using buckets and bowls to transport water from the hydrant. Lurie hoped they'd be able to put fish into the moat eventually.

She was startled from these thoughts by the click of the gate latch. Mack Baird appeared, a finger pressed to his lips. He'd been really annoying lately, always standing too close with his sweaty, boy smell. The other day, they were wrestling on the grass, and he stayed on top of her until she couldn't breathe and almost started crying. Kizzy made fun of her but for a few seconds, Lurie had been really afraid.

She stood up and he was next to her, alongside the tall fence that divided her yard from the neighbors'.

"You got me," she said. But when she tried to pass by, he grabbed her arm.

"Let's hide together," he said. His breath smelled like wet potato chips.

"But they already found you."

He kept hold of her arm and pulled her against his chest.

"Stop it," she said.

Pushing her against the fence, breathing and leaning, both hands on her arms now, turning her, squeezing.

"Kizzy!" she yelled, but then his hand clamped over her mouth. She licked it, tasted salt and dirt.

He smiled and wiped his palm against her cheek.

She wriggled and fought, leaning her head back as the blue sky bared down, as the fence creaked and cracked from the pressure.

"There you are."

Kizzy and Billy pushed through the gate. Kizzy's brow crinkled when she saw them.

Mack released her. "She wins again," he said.

"Let's work on the river," Billy said. He wiped his nose with the back of his hand.

Lurie noticed there was a smear of dirt on the younger kid's forehead, the same smear that had been there yesterday. Mrs. Baird never came outside to check on the boys like their mom did. In fact, Lurie seldom saw either of their parents.

Mack whacked his brother on the back of the head. "It's a *moat*, dummy."

Then, as though in response to some unheard signal, they all began to run. Lurie had a lead on Kizzy at first but was soon overtaken. Kizzy had always been stronger and faster, and she couldn't tolerate her younger sister winning anything.

Lurie ran on anyway, happy for the fresh, grassy smell and the cool air that lifted the hair from her neck. Her legs were warm and pliant and fast. Around the house, down a long stretch of sidewalk, to the end of the street where the yellow hydrant sat in the middle. And the last thing she remembered, later, stretched out on the white, white sheets with her mother looking down, was the feeling of sliding on a pond, skating or gliding, maybe the final anticipation before flying, and the blue sky was all around, the trees a blur of heft and space, the water splashing onto her arms, which reached and waved against the endless air before everything went black.

A Family Reunion

Glen Hanley dipped his fingers into the glass of tepid water and rubbed his temples. The letters and numbers on the sheet before him pulsed and expanded, indecipherable. Some of his friends, men his age, had started wearing reading glasses. Usually small-framed with square lenses, always perched on the tips of their noses as they hunched over a newspaper or a restaurant menu. Glen Hanley did not want reading glasses.

"Good morning."

He looked up and waited for his eyes to focus on Jody Beauford, a new loan officer who had transferred from the La Mirada branch. She posed in the frame of the office door, her backside turned his way in a bright red skirt, round and smooth as an apple.

"Morning, Jody." He straightened up in his chair and squared his shoulders.

She leaned back, allowing a peek of her fitted, gray sweater. "Good weekend?"

"Soccer games," he said. "My daughter's team won second place in a tournament. We were there most of Saturday."

Her lips stretched into a reluctant smile. "That's great," she said. And before he could ask about her weekend, she had disappeared.

Glen Hanley had never played soccer. His mother signed him up for baseball once, but they never seemed to make it to the practices and when he did show up for games, the coach stuck him in right field and made him bat last. He quit after one season. In junior high, he tried out for basketball, because he was already quite tall by then, but he lacked coordination and drive. It wasn't until high school when he joined the cross-country team that he found something he could do alone and do well.

He'd tried to encourage his daughters. Kizzy was sinewy and fast, a natural athlete, but Lurie was built more like Janet—pear-shaped, with little muscle tone in her arms and legs. Both girls had tried softball and tennis, soccer and volleyball. Swimming lessons and gymnastics. None of it stuck with Lurie, but Kizzy still played soccer in the fall and softball every spring. She was twelve and Lurie had just turned ten.

Glen Hanley wanted to be a good dad. His remembrances of his own father, who left when he was seven, were muddled and scant. Broad shoulders over a seatback, oil ground into the crevices of his hands, the roar of his car from the garage. His mother had kept the office job at the auto rebuilding shop where Glen's parents met; eventually, she became the manager. Glen and his sisters, who were just three when their father took off, got used to fending for themselves.

His phone buzzed, a dull, mechanical sound. A single ring: someone inside the bank.

He picked it up. "Yes?"

"It's Bret." Another loan officer, mostly mortgages like Glen. "The Crestfield loan, will it be ready to fund by Thursday?"

"Should be," Glen said. "Waiting for financials on that—" He shuffled papers on his desk, "—what was it, a boat?"

"Yeah, sailboat."

"Jesus," he said. "Anyway, should be good to go."

Bret was part of the bank foursome, tennis at the club every Tuesday and Thursday. They'd been playing for a few years. The sport came easily for Glen, perhaps because of his years of running, perhaps because he'd been meant to play it all along. Sometimes he wished he could go back to high school and try for the tennis team.

"Thanks," Bret said. "Hey, is she still there?"

"Who?"

"Jody."

Glen looked at the red telephone light, now static. "What? No."

"Have you talked to Steve?"

"Steve?"

A shuffling sound, a shifting. Bret seemed to have covered part of his telephone receiver when he spoke again. "Some of the guys went for happy hour on Friday. He says Jody came home with him."

An image of Steve came to mind, throwing a football at the bank picnic the preceding summer. Tank top, tanned arms. "I thought he was married," Glen said.

"Wife's away with the kids."

"Jesus."

"Yeah," Bret said.

Glen's second line lit up. Another call. "You believe that?" he asked.

"Sure, happens all the time."

When Bret hung up, Glen Hanley heard the sound two-fold, in the ear holding his own telephone and from Bret's office three doors down. An echo, a time-lapse.

His telephone rang again, two quick buzzes. An outside call.

"Union Bank. Glen Hanley speaking."

"Is this Glen Albert Hanley?"

He flinched, a vision of the metal toolbox gathering dust in his mother's garage, "Albert" scratched across the top. "Yes. This is the loan department of Union Bank."

The woman cleared her throat. "My name is Penny Daniels. Penny like money, Daniels like the boy in the lion's den. I'm calling from Plain Township, Ohio."

"I'm sorry, you've reached the Union Bank in Bellflower, California. Do you have a wrong number?"

"Well, I'm not sure."

Glen looked down at the paperwork placed squarely in the corner of his desk. Rows of orderly numbers, clear facts. "Ma'am, I don't understand."

"Glen Albert Hanley, born in San Francisco on March 14—"

"Who is this?"

"I believe I'm your sister, Glen. My daddy is, was, Albert Rosedale Hanley."

Elbows on desk, he leaned towards the telephone. "He's dead?"

"Sorry, no. I don't know. Dead to us, I guess."

"Us?"

The woman took a deep breath. "I'm mishandling this, Glen. I'm sorry. Have you talked to your dad?"

"No." His eyes swam. "Would you hold on for a moment?"

"Sure."

Glen Hanley stood up, his eyes darting around to familiar things. A photograph of Janet and the girls, the wooden pencil holder painted by Lurie, a Union Bank flip calendar. He walked to the opening of his office and looked around the lobby of the bank. The usual early morning business. Elderly mostly, an occasional suit. He went back to his desk. "Sorry about that," he said into the receiver. "What was your name again?"

"Penny Daniels," she answered. "My mother is Diana Daniels, maiden name Porterhouse but that doesn't matter to you. Your dad and my mom were married for seven years. There are two of us, my sister and me. Sherry. That's my sister."

Glen's fingers grazed the surface of the water in his drinking glass, tracing circles. "You're in Ohio?"

"Yes. Are you about forty-one?"

"Forty-two," he said.

"I'm thirty-five," Penny said. "And Sherry is thirty-two."

"My sisters are thirty-eight," Glen told her. "Twins." He felt more comfortable with this part of the conversation, doing the math. "He certainly didn't waste any time."

She clicked her tongue. "No, I guess not."

"Where is he now?"

"Heaven only knows. As I said, they were married seven years. He left when I was five. Much the same as what he did to you, I guess."

"And you've never heard from him?"

"Nope."

"What about your mother?"

"Hmph. We'd hear about it if she had. Not a lot of understanding in her heart for that man." There was a slight accent in her voice. He couldn't place it. He'd never been to the Midwest, but he supposed that's what it was.

Glen Hanley shook his head, letting the image sink in of another family, a déjà vu of his life occurring unbeknownst to him in Ohio. "How did you find me?" he asked.

"My mother gave me some papers with your names. I just searched for you in California on the internet."

He remembered posing for a photograph out in the parking lot on a hot day. In the picture, his eyes were almost squinted shut. "The bank website," he said.

"Right," she said. "I could email you photos, I mean, if you're interested what we look like."

"I don't know."

"That's all right," she said.

"Your sisters were pretty small when he left?" she asked.

"Three years old," he said.

"Where do they live now?"

He wiped his wet fingers on his pant leg. "I'm not sure they'd want to know about this. I'll talk to them."

"Oh, I wouldn't call them," she said. "I'll leave that to you. The oldest in a family should decide, right?"

And Glen Hanley's defensive side rose up, his practicality. "What do you want, uh, Penny? I haven't seen him in thirty-five years. My mother is deceased."

"I'm sorry to hear that, Glen."

"Thank you." His face flushed. His mother, battling for so long, His father, that bastard. "I can't help you. I have nothing."

"It's not like that, Glen. I thought maybe I could help you."

Bret appeared in the doorway. Huddled around the telephone, Glen lifted a hand and waved him away. Bret nodded and left, although his eyebrows rose.

"You must have wondered," she said, "if it was something you'd done. I know I did. Maybe you thought he was killed or kidnapped. I thought all those things until I found out about you. I'd go back and forth, one to the other, hating him and worrying about him. Then I realized it was *his* fault, some wrong part of *him*. Who could leave a woman with young children, just drop off the face of the planet? And then do it again?" She sighed, a long whoosh of air. "Shoot, maybe there's more kids out there somewhere."

Glen's large hand gripped the edge of his desk until the knuckles were white. Then, just as quickly, he let go. "It's almost—" He stopped, wordless.

A pause on the line, two hearts beating. Business in the bank continued. Checks deposited, balances verified, money transferred. Cars and houses and boats. Saving and spending, adding and subtracting. Resources moving from place to place, intangible, innumerable. Glen Hanley dipped his fingers into the lukewarm water and brought them to his forehead, his eyes seeking out the balance sheet beneath him.

CHAPTER

5

Moore

Woman Fears for Her Life

Blues and greens and whites, many shades of white. Tubes, cloths, digital screens blinking and blinking. The room is space, light, astringent smells. In one corner, a television tuned to a golf tournament, tiny men on grassy hills.

The plastic bracelet makes a soft sucking sound when she pulls it away from her wrist. They've given her something, she remembers. Something to relax.

"That's my wife," Tyler said when questioned by a nurse. My wife, my wife. Seven years now, the seven-year itch.

Amber presses her head into the soft pillow, which rises to surround her neck. One quick surgery and done with it. Done with it. Her mother, having the nerve to suggest fertility treatments could have caused it. I'm thirty-eight, Mom. Nothing but bad luck to blame here.

Tyler touches her arm. Her husband, her sweet husband. He's been so patient. Hard to believe how their story started, but here they are.

"How are you feeling?" he asks.

"Fuzzy," she says through thick lips.

He leans down and kisses her forehead. "That's good, I think."

"Where did the girls go?"

"Snack machine," he says and as if on cue, they appear in the doorway. Joy in jeans and a shirt that shows her navel, a streak of purple hair over her left ear. And Melinda, whom Amber had wanted to name "Hope" but thought it would be too corny.

"They're out of pretzels," Joy says. At fifteen, she's thin and toned from years of dance classes, which she has recently quit.

Melinda runs forward, a bag of M&Ms extended. "Mommy, look." She has just turned four. They had a party at Chuck E. Cheese. Amber's mother arranged the whole thing. Her parents, still taking care of her after all this time.

Tyler scoops up Melinda. "Mommy can't have any of those, Mel."

"Save some," Amber tries to say, but it comes out warbled. Her husband's eyes narrow, and he hurries the girls back out to their grandmother in the waiting room. Amber hadn't wanted them at the hospital, but Tyler had insisted. It'll be easier, he said, if they know where you've gone.

Her eyes flood when she sees him now, looking at her with such concern. She wonders if he will love her the same, as promised, with or without breasts, and whether or not they are able to have more children. But she feels the assurance of his hand as she closes her eyes.

Boy Fears for His Life

Daddy's waiting in the car when I come out. His eyes are shiny and wet like he's already thinking about the water. My nose is cold, my fingers are cold. Steam is coming from a pipe underneath the truck, and the boards are already strapped in. He did that last night when the truck was still in the garage. Mommy had to move her craft stuff out of the way so he could get the truck all the way in. She likes to make these books that have a bunch of pictures of us, then she writes things and adds decorations. Sometimes she goes to meetings where a bunch of moms do the books together. Daddy thinks she spends too much time on them and calls them "crapbooks" instead of "scrapbooks" to make us laugh.

"Let's go," he says. "Water's churning." His face is red from the morning. The white parts of his eyes are a little red, too.

"What's that?" I ask.

"Churning," he says. "Like a big stew." He pokes his finger into my ribs, but I can barely feel it through the wetsuit. "Just waiting for two pieces of meat."

I don't really want to think about being a piece of meat in the ocean. I mean, there are sharks, and I heard a girl got a piece of her ass chewed off last summer.

"What happened to the girl last summer?" I ask.

Daddy reaches over to turn down the radio because it's all static. "What girl?"

"There was a shark," I say. "She got bit in her, her *backside*." I use the word my mom likes better than the others.

He laughs. "Tyler, the sharks aren't gonna bother you. You know that."

"I know."

"Sometimes you need to shut your brain down, quit worrying so much. You're eight years old."

"Almost nine," I say. I tuck my hands under my armpits, but the suit feels cold. "Can you turn up the heater?"

We live really close to the beach, so it doesn't take long. There are a few cars when we get there. We park right next to the bathrooms because I usually have to go one last time before we get in. Mommy says I have a nervous bladder. Daddy makes fun of me and says I should just go in the water. But the wetsuit is tight, and you end up with legs full of pee. It's gross.

The sun is a fat yellow and white smear at the edge of the ocean. It looks like the finger paint we used in kindergarten. We don't do that anymore. In second grade, you use paintbrushes for art.

Daddy's board is a long one, with a green stripe down the middle and a sharp fin on the bottom. I know it's sharp because one time, I helped carry it and the fin cut my shoulder. Mommy was mad about that. She doesn't like to surf, and she doesn't like it when me and Karly go. She's not a good swimmer, and she thinks the sun and salt are bad for our skin.

My board is small, and it has red and white decorations. I got it for Christmas even though I wanted a new bicycle. It's shiny and light and the perfect size for me. I hate it.

"Come here." Daddy smears zinc under each of my eyes. I can see myself in his sunglasses before he takes them off and locks them in the glove box. They're expensive, he tells us all the time.

"Mommy already put sunscreen," I tell him.

"I know she did." He looks at the water then back at me. "But we can't be too careful, right?" His eyes are saying that we have a secret together, that it's just us guys.

I'd be happy to stop here, to skip the next part and get to the fried eggs and toast at the café. They have a silver thing that holds about ten different kinds of jelly. The waitresses are nice, and they bring extra hot chocolate even when you don't ask. But first, we have to surf.

The water is freezing where it gets me on my hands and neck. I hate when it creeps into the suit like little bugs. We wade in, and then we're floating. I haven't come out with Daddy for a while, so he sticks close to me.

"Tyler, paddle," he says, because I stopped for a minute. Lying on the board, the sun feels good on my back. If only I could just float and watch him. Why can't I just watch him?

"Here comes one for you," he says, and I know which wave he means right away. Small with edges like light and smooth in the middle. A beginner's wave. I paddle faster, catching and even passing him a little. I get on the wave too late and come crashing down.

"Good try," he says when I swim back. There's a look on his face, like he's not very happy.

We stay together for a few more, then he says he's going out far. There are some men out there, and I know he wants to talk to them and have a better ride.

That makes me mad because I could be home in my warm bed like Karly. My mom says she's too young to go unless we're all in the water, Daddy watching me and her with Karly. So I have to go by myself. But when we get here, he goes out with the other stupid surfers, all of them with their long hair and stupid loud voices.

I start to paddle quickly, my hands like the propeller of a boat, slapping the water. I go out farther and farther. I can see Daddy in the distance. And there it is, my wave. Bigger than the beginner waves but smooth. Strong-looking. I know I can do it. I've had years of swimming lessons and surfing camp three summers in a row. I paddle, and I see Daddy paddling, too. Maybe we can catch the same wave and wouldn't he like that, to look over and see me.

I get on my feet and feel the board pull forward. It's fast, too fast, and before I can dive, I'm under water, turning and turning. The ocean is all around, white and mean. I think about sharks and raspberry jelly, and Mommy. I see my feet like they aren't my feet anymore. The water is loud and quiet at the same time, churning and churning. And then Daddy is there, his green swimming trunks puffing around his legs, his hand squeezing my arm and pulling, and everything changing as we get closer to air.

Girl Fears for Her Life

Joy emerges from the dance floor, a sea of warmth and pulse, and looks for her drink. There are a few circular tables pushed against the wall, each crowded with smeared glasses and bottles. Impossible to know which is hers. She stands near a group of guys—gelled hair, studded belts, heavy cologne—and knows she is not their type. She really needs a drink.

Someone grabs her elbow. "What the hell?" Rania yells into her ear.

Joy backs up. "What?"

"I've been looking for you." She flips her hair over one shoulder. "Kieran's here. He's outside."

Joy wobbles a bit, her heart slowing after the dance session. The floor pulses up through her shoes, all bass. "I need a drink first."

Rania reaches over and wipes something from Joy's cheek. She purses her lips. "Those boys left."

By "boys," she means the high schoolers buying Joy drinks all night, happy to use their fake IDs and watch her dance. She thinks she may have kissed one of them. She remembers pushing against him during a long mix, bodies bouncing and then, an unbelievable move she made, arching her back and stepping backwards as they cleared out of the way. They were young, she realizes. She and Rania have fake IDs also, but at least they're not in high school anymore.

Rania's not happy. She grabs both of Joy's arms and steadies her. "Get some water," she says. "Then meet me outside."

Joy breaks free and walks to the bar. She squeezes in alongside a huge dude with hairy arms. He looks down her shirt. She motions him over, and he leans his head slightly toward her. "Sorry," she says into his meaty ear. "I'm just so thirsty, and my friend left with my purse."

His eyebrows rise, thick as his fingers, which surround his glass and are almost as hairy.

She waits. Nothing. She waves him over again and asks, "Do you have a couple dollars I could borrow?"

"Sure," he says, his mouth opening to huge teeth. He raises a hand, the bartender appears and within a few moments, two shot glasses are placed before her.

"Thanks." She pushes one toward him.

He shakes his head, and one of his huge hands rests on the small of her back. "You have both."

Joy slams the first one, something sweet, while his hand finds the side of her hip. After the second, he pulls her to the dance floor. She owes him this, she knows, and the music is pumping and the bodies part to let them in, and she doesn't mind for a while, the swaying, the sparkling lights, the sweat trickling down her spine. The beat takes over, becomes her pulse. She is fading, falling. Her mind makes lyrics for the song: I'm not this girl, I'm not this girl. She leans against him, gives him his money's worth.

Rania elbows a small blonde and grabs Joy's arm. They make their escape, around the endless rows and formations of people, through the door that has been propped open to let in air. Outside, around a corner, three guys lean against the gray brick building. Kieran stands in the middle, his blonde hair covering one eye and his lips dark and ruddy. A little blue pill sits on the palm of his extended hand.

Joy stumbles toward the group, sadness at her back like a pressing wind; despite the blur and blend she knows what it means, what she will have, what she will owe, her thoughts crowding and the black night all around. Rania hands her a bottle of water and the coolness floods her throat and chases the blue pill. And in that brief moment, Joy is loved and nurtured, and has everything she needs.

CHAPTER

6

Hallowicz

Woman Seeks Comfort

"Jesus H. Christ," Mrs. Hallowicz said. She bent her neck from side to side, trying to release the tightness. "Must have slept wrong."

In the kitchen, light streamed through the windows. She trudged to the cabinet and took down the bottle of pain relievers. One side of her neck was stiff, the tendon underneath like a rope that had been pulled and tied to some part of her shoulder. Sometimes, the pain shot down her arm.

She made a cup of tea, which seemed to help. In her neat bedroom, she put on a green cardigan and hung her nightdress on the bedpost. She ran a brush through her hair, which was still shiny and held some curl, even at her age. "Jesus H. Christ," she said again, and thought of her mother. Belted dresses and hats with delicate lace visors, red lipstick and red fingernails. Her mother wouldn't appreciate the Lord's name being taken, although to Mrs. Hallowicz it wasn't "in vain." Surely, this was as good a time as any.

She went to the living room and lowered herself onto the couch. The upholstery was tweed, scratchy even through her slacks. She never sat on the couch, preferring her recliner. But there was a telephone on the end table, and she wouldn't make the call from the kitchen. "F, G, H," she muttered, until she found the correct page in her address book. She cleared her throat and dialed.

Rob and Kathy had moved around quite a bit over the years, so Mrs. Hallowicz never bothered to memorize their phone number. Kathy had some sort of office job, and Rob was an engineer for the electric company. One thing she could say about her son, he had always worked hard. Kathy, on the other hand, was never happy. She changed jobs frequently and made Rob buy one house after the other in places with strange names—Angel Fire, Taos, Agua Fria. Within a few years, they'd move again. Mrs. Hallowicz had visited them once in New Mexico, years ago. The twins were about ten years old then, both with the same strawberry-blonde hair Robbie had as a kid, both knobby-kneed and gap-toothed.

"Where are they now?" Mrs. Hallowicz asked aloud. She hadn't heard from her grandchildren, Joshua and Amanda, for a long time. No Christmas cards, nothing on her birthday. Kathy signed their names as if they were still children. "Last I heard, they're both in college, draining money and giving nothing back." She shook her head. "And now there's the other one."

She pressed the buttons slowly, one at a time. A few staccato rings, muffled sounds, then her son's clear voice: "Hello?"

"Robbie," she started, but her voice failed. She tried again. "Rob."

"Mom? Is everything okay?"

"Why wouldn't it be?" she said.

"Well, I don't know."

More voices in the background, a woman's, a child's.

"Hold on, Mom. Kathy's getting ready to leave." He covered the mouthpiece, but she could still hear. "I know what I said, but they've changed it to tonight. Call me when you get there." Then, Kathy's voice, indecipherable. "All right, all right," Rob said. "You said that. Good luck, Steven. See you there."

Mrs. Hallowicz's heart clenched. "Rob?"

"Sorry, Mom. I'm back." He exhaled and adjusted the telephone. She could picture him, settling into a chair, his belly resting on his lap, sweating probably.

"How's your weather?" she asked.

"Warm," he said. "You?"

"Hot," she said. "My azaleas are suffering."

"Your air conditioning's working?"

"I would hope so. Three thousand dollars!" She'd had to replace the unit several years back, and Rob had helped her deal with the salesman.

"That included the extra work," he reminded her. "It's an old house, everything's getting old."

Her neck was killing her. She moved the receiver to the other ear and pressed her fingers into the tight tendon. "When will that ibuprofen kick in?" she said.

"What?"

She blinked. "Nothing, nothing. Where's Kathy going?"

"Today?"

"Now."

"Steven's got a soccer game. Actually, I gotta head out soon. She's angry I can't make the pizza party afterwards."

"Why can't you?"

He sniffed. "Poker night."

"You still do that?"

"I enjoy it."

She sniffed back. "I know you do." What she thought was: You should be able to do what you want, Rob, and you're too old to start over. She didn't know what he and Kathy had been thinking having another child at their ages. The twins had to be almost twenty-one by now and here they were, saddled with another one to raise. Mrs. Hallowicz was certain it'd been Kathy's idea. Robbie was fifty-three years old. They should be winding down, maybe traveling or playing in a bowling league. Things she would have liked to do with Wilson. There's an order to life, she thought.

"Listen, Robbie," she said. "I have something to tell you." His house was quiet now, and Mrs. Hallowicz wished Kathy was there after all. To be alone and get such news—

"Mom, what?"

She cleared her throat, rubbed her neck. "Gordon died."

"Who?"

"Gordon," she said. "Collapsed. I had to call someone to make sure. Who knows how old he was. You remember how we came to have him. There's just no telling, Robbie. But he's gone."

"My God," he said. "You mean the turtle?"

"Yes," she snapped. "Your pet. He died."

"Okay, Mom. I'm sorry to hear that."

Savagely, she wiped her hand across her face. "He was very smart, you know."

"Yeah," Rob said. "Remember the time he ran really fast?"

She closed her eyes. Her Robbie. So naïve. "I never saw anything like that."

"Well, he did."

In the kitchen, the refrigerator hummed. Outside, a car sped by, too quickly.

"What did you do with him?" Rob asked.

Fatigue spread over Mrs. Hallowicz like a warm blanket. The pain in her neck was lessening but another was starting, something deep-rooted and familiar, something that could choke her if she let it. Her boy, her Stevie. How long had it been? "What could I do?" she said. "I had to bury him."

Man Suffers Loss of Loved One

Kathy stomped around the house, making noise wherever she went. Rob heard her keys jangle onto a table, then a cupboard slamming, then a door. He closed his eyes and opened them. Rubbing his hand in a circular motion on the bathroom mirror, he cleared a space. The comb did quick work; his hair was thinning at an alarming rate. You've got a nicely shaped head for it, Kathy told him once, and he'd always thought it was a particularly kind thing for her to say.

She'd been mostly unhappy with him for some time. He never knew when it would hit, and her reactions often seemed overblown. This pizza party, for instance. Why in the world did she care so much about it? She'd never minded his monthly poker nights in the past. In fact, he thought she enjoyed having a night to herself once in a while. Impossible, he said to his reflection.

In the hallway, he passed Steven, who held one red sock in his hand.

"Dad, have you seen the other one?" he asked, holding it aloft.

"Sorry, no." Rob ruffled his son's hair, thinking as he did what a cliché thing it was to do. "Look in the dryer, and you'd better hurry."

They exchanged a look. She's in a mood, it said.

Kathy wasted no time once he was in the kitchen. She stood at the counter, methodically swallowing her supplements. White, blue, orange, and green pills in a variety of shapes and sizes. All natural. All to help with "the transition," as she liked to call it. "You told me several times it was next weekend," she said. "I don't understand when this happened."

"I'm sorry," he said. Opening the refrigerator, he stared inside.

"Didn't you just have lunch?" she asked.

"I'm looking for one of those juice drinks you bought me," he lied.

"In the bottom drawer." She put her empty glass into the dishwasher. "The game should only go 'til five-thirty. We'll be done with pizza by seven-thirty. Can't you go to poker a little late?"

He shut the door and turned to her. "I've been to hundreds of pizza parties. Skip it if you don't want to go." As she reached under the sink for the dishwasher detergent, he had a carnal thought and wondered, realistically, what his chances would be after the poker party. Maybe ten percent, he thought.

When she straightened up, her face was red. "You've been to Josh and Amanda's soccer parties, years ago. I acknowledge that. But it's not like you earned a pass for Steven's. He needs us, too."

She was starting to get to him. Many rebuttals occurred to him, but he pushed them down. The worst one brought shame because he loved Steven and couldn't imagine life without him. He opened his mouth then closed it again.

The telephone rang, startling them both. Kathy turned on her heel and as he picked it up, she went into the bathroom. From the family room, Steven yelled: "I found it! I found the other one!"

"Hello?"

Some mumbling, then "Robbie?"

Her voice sounded strange. "Mom," he said. "Is everything okay?"

"Why wouldn't it be?"

There she was, he thought, back to herself. The whole history of his neglect in her question, the insinuation that she was fine, just fine, without him.

"I don't know," he said.

Kathy came back through the kitchen. Steven trailed behind her, throwing a soccer ball up every few steps. She walked right past Rob to the door. He could smell her perfume. He asked his mother to hold on. "Kathy. I know what I said, but they've changed it to tonight." He rubbed her shoulder, and he could feel her soften, just a little.

"Call me when you get there?"

She stood on tiptoe and brushed her lips across his cheek. Then she whispered "Asshole" in his ear, but she was smiling.

"I can't believe you said that," he said, winking at his son. "Good luck, Steven." Then he ducked as Kathy tried to smack him.

"Robbie?"

"Sorry, Mom. I'm back." He watched his wife and son through the window. Steven picked up a stray rock from their front yard—if a yard could consist of a blanket of stones instead of grass, that is.

"How's your weather?" his mother asked.

"Warm," he said.

He knew she wanted him to say that it was hot, that it was always hot, although he'd explained to her many times that they lived in a mild part of New Mexico, with a forest and river nearby. They even got snow in the winter sometimes. But she wouldn't listen, would not picture his state as anything other than desert and Indians, even though she had visited when they lived in Angel Fire.

They talked about her weather, which was killing her flowers, she said, and she complained about the price of her air conditioning unit. He had spent several hours on the telephone dealing with that situation when it arose a few years ago. His mother was so worried she'd be taken advantage of but really, he couldn't imagine anyone pulling one over on her. She was as tough as you get.

"Where's Kathy going?" she asked now.

"Today?" He prepared himself for the follow-up, which would probably be something about Kathy's "new job," even though she had been at the same title company for six years. What his mother remembered were the years before that, when Kathy had been laid off twice.

Her voice was impatient. "Now."

"Steven's got a soccer game." He glanced at the clock, wondering if he'd have time to get the oil changed in his truck before it started. "Actually, I gotta head out soon. She's angry I can't make the pizza party afterwards." Subconsciously, he kicked himself.

"Why can't you?"

"Poker night," he said.

She coughed. "You still do that?"

"I enjoy it."

"I know you do. Listen, Robbie. I have something to tell you."

"Okay," he said. For some reason, he thought about his brother. He always thought about his brother whenever someone said they had news, or something to say, although no one on this earth could have anything to say about his brother now, because he'd been gone for forty-seven years. The old woman had grown quiet. "Mom, what?"

"Gordon died."

He searched his mind. Did his mother have any friends left? What was her doctor's name, the one with the sailboat? Did the Gleesons still live next door? Was it Mr. Gleeson? His mother was rambling now, he couldn't understand her. Slowly, it dawned on him. "My God," he said. "You mean the turtle?"

"Yes, your pet. He died." She was almost yelling.

"Okay, Mom." He remembered building the cage with his father, watching the turtle from time to time until eventually, he forgot all about it. "I'm sorry to hear that," he told her.

"He was very smart, you know."

Rob did recall one thing, the reason he called him Flash Gordon. "Remember the time he ran really fast?"

"I never saw anything like that."

Too late, he remembered that she had never believed him. The times she made him feel foolish and small and doubt himself. "Well, he did," he said. Her endless chores, washing, cooking, walking through the house until his father called to her. "Get out here, Betsy! Life's passing you by!"

He felt a real urge now. He'd drive straight to the game; he'd tell the guys he'd be a little late to poker. Starting tomorrow, he'd call his mother more often, maybe they'd even plan a trip to visit her for the holidays. Steven hadn't been to California since he was a baby. He thought he heard a sniffle, and he pressed the telephone against his ear. If his mother had called about the turtle, he realized, it must be big news to her. "What did you do with him?" he asked.

"What could I do?" she said. Implication: *you weren't here*. "I had to bury him."

"I'm sorry," Rob said. "I'm really sorry." And he pictured the old woman with a shovel, parting the packed dirt, dust rising in a cloud around the hem of her faded housedress. "I'm sorry," he said again, because there was nothing else to do.

CHAPTER

7

Hanley/Gleeson

A Love Affair

Susan parked her car on the side of the building under a lone palm tree. Cream-colored with a vaguely Spanish arch in front, the hotel looked like any other mid-range, California hotel across from a shopping center. La Quinta Inn & Suites in Hawaiian Gardens was four stories high, just fifty-three rooms, seven of which were suites. Check-in after three p.m., check-out at noon, standard. According to the hotel's website, they offered a free breakfast, although she wouldn't be around to enjoy that. And as she always did, Susan wondered who decided to name a California town "Hawaiian Gardens."

Reaching up, she flipped down the sun visor and checked her makeup in the mirror. Her eye shadow glittered in the afternoon sun; her golden-blonde hair was still curled nicely. She remembered when she and Glen had met for an official date, and he'd been relieved to see her hair. Because the other first time, the party, the groping and licking next to the long, creaky fence—her face heated to think of it now—she'd been wearing the wig. He said later he wasn't sure what color her natural hair was.

She craned her neck, looking for his Toyota amidst the cars already parked. Just a few, non-descript autos here and there and a rusted-out and dented green El Camino that probably belonged to one of the employees. La Quinta wasn't the epitome of class, but it was a sight better than the Holiday Inn in La Mirada. The last time they'd been there, the young hotel clerk with the pointy nose and long nails made a sarcastic comment about fresh towels and Susan told Glen she'd never set foot in the place again. Smart-ass young girl, what did she know about anything?

From its awkward beginnings—the party, the escape—the thing between them had progressed to a more respectable level, she thought. They were grownups, and although a mid-afternoon meeting at an affordable hotel was completely unoriginal, it was all they could do. Guilt surfaced at times, defiance at others. It had been her husband's fiftieth birthday party, after all. She'd planned it for months—the food, the invitation list, even the *theme*, for God's sake—and the image of she and Glen tearing at each other's clothes against that beat-up fence wasn't her proudest memory. When he had called her cell phone the next afternoon, she'd been flattered and anxious. Nobody can explain exactly what it feels like when a entire new possibility presents itself, like a hole opening in the ground that was once all layers of dirt and tangled roots.

Glen had found Susan's personal number by looking through the contacts on his wife's phone. Then he went out for a drive, an errand to buy some Tylenol for his hangover, he told Janet. He pulled over and called, said he had to see her, that he'd been thinking of nothing else for the past twelve hours and despite several hands-on efforts, he'd been unable to keep away the pounding erection that filled his shorts each and every time he thought about her breasts in the red satin dress.

Susan and her husband had never been very vocal in the sack, so the directness of this proclamation both embarrassed and titillated her. He seemed like a very decisive and manly sort of man, this Glen Hanley, and some passive, soft womanly part of her thawed and acquiesced. There was a sort of relief in it, feeling as though he was making the decisions and she couldn't do much to stop it, to stop him.

A tapping sound startled her from her thoughts. The sunlight was coming almost horizontally now, gleaming between two palm trees above the arch of the hotel, making her blink and blink until she made out Glen's face in its shadow. She smiled and opened the door. He pulled her from the car, and his hands were on her back, the tips of his fingers already pressing under the waistband of her shorts. It was late September but still hot, too usual in California to be called an Indian summer.

"You look great," he said.

She looked down at the outfit she'd chosen, white shorts and a pale pink t-shirt studded with sparkles along the neckline. She noticed he still wore his work clothes—navy slacks, dress shirt loosened and wrinkled at the elbows. He looked worn in.

The lobby was roomy, and their steps echoed. Behind the counter, the wall was painted a dark plum color; the sofas and chairs scattered about were patterned, scrolls and flowers, in similar dark colors. Better to hide stains, Susan thought.

The tall man behind the desk looked up. "Checking in?"

She crossed her arms over her chest; the air conditioning was having an effect on her.

They waited while the clerk punched buttons on his computer. "Breakfast is included," he finally said. "We serve an assortment of cereals and breads, or you can make your own waffle. Right here in the lobby, starts at seven a.m."

"Sounds great," Glen said. He lifted her bag, a white leather duffle, and his own, which made a clinking sound she knew to be caused by a bottle of wine and two glasses. "Ready, sweetie?"

Sweetie? Where had that come from? She followed him to the elevator, where a long crack in a nearby baseboard distracted her from what he was saying.

"Susan."

She blinked again. "Sorry, yes?"

"Is everything okay?" he asked.

She stood on tiptoe and nuzzled her mouth into his neck, imagining that even this small gesture was causing him to be aroused. There was a power in it, in her.

At first, the sex had been frantic and intense. They had decided to meet for drinks one night when Doug had a business dinner and Glen was supposed to be at tennis. It had been three days since the party but no opportunity had arisen to slip away sooner. During that time, Susan cancelled plans then made them again, over and over and always just in her mind. This is that moment, she told herself, the moment where a marriage changes, a wife faces a fork in the road. And sometimes, a different thought would occur to her, that Glen himself would cancel, or change his mind, or not be attracted to her after all in the bright light of regular life. Somehow, amidst all the uncertainty, she kept the plans, maybe just to find out what would happen.

They met at an Olive Garden in Cerritos. From the start, they had to get out of Bellflower, had to think about running into PTA friends and coworkers, anyone who could connect them back to their marriages, their children. Glen sat with his back turned at the bar. She remembered how his presence had increased as she approached. And when he stretched to his full stature, his broad shoulders, his muscled arms, she had to restrain herself from burrowing into his chest. Two martinis each, an appetizer of potato skins, and his hand was creeping between her legs under the muslin skirt. She held his other hand, her right and his right, their elbows on the bar as though they were arm wrestling, and his left hand, his fingers, somehow reached her.

They finished in the parking lot, no time to get anywhere else. They moved his car to the back of the lot next to the trash bins, and she mounted him in the driver's seat, oblivious to the minor bruises and scrapes that were sure to follow. They weren't kids, after all.

They met once more for drinks, then Glen shyly suggested the Holiday Inn. It became a routine. He would text her suggesting a day, either one of his tennis evenings, or an afternoon he could get out of work. They'd synch schedules and meet, usually in time for a three o'clock check-in, back home by eight or nine. She didn't know how Glen managed it with his kids still at home. Hers were grown, all living independently now, even Sandy, whom they had worried about most of all. Ryan was in the valley, drawing animation for a film company, and Kristopher had stayed in Michigan after college and law school. Sandy had recently returned from northern California and seemed to be much more stable. She'd found a job as a pet groomer and had aspirations to start her own business. None of them had married yet, but Kristopher had been with Violet for some time. Susan didn't worry. Just because she had gotten hitched at a ridiculously young age, had started having children at nineteen—that wasn't how it was done anymore. Her oldest, Ryan, was twenty-nine, but that wasn't as old as it used to be.

She sat on the bedspread, darkly patterned like the furniture downstairs, and watched Glen open the Merlot. She wondered whether they could manage an afternoon without it. There were two double beds, and she moved over to his. She crawled behind him and pressed her chest against his broad back. She ran her fingers through his hair.

"Almost got it," he said. He pulled the cork and only half came out. The broken portion remained in the bottle's neck. "Shit!" His body tensed beneath her.

"It's all right," she said. "I may not have any."

"What? Oh." He leaned over and put the bottle next to the glasses on the small table that jutted out between the beds. Then he turned towards her and lifted her shirt.

They always started this way. His fascination with her breasts had continued, and she could only guess it was because Janet's were so small, although she had a nice figure, anyway. Susan shook her head. Thinking about Glen's wife wouldn't get anything accomplished.

His mouth clamped onto her nipple, and she had a vague thought about breastfeeding. They'd been such hippies then, she and Doug. He was getting his contracting business off the ground, and they were all young, he and his partners. They hung out on the weekends, and it became like a family, the wives and kids too, barbecues and swim parties. And Susan thought nothing of pulling out a breast to feed one of her babies. The kids came quickly, one after the other;

probably all of their acquaintances had grown quite tired of her breasts in those years.

Glen was licking now, his tongue making circular motions as his hand found its way to her crotch. He was a little awkward in this area, sometimes a bit too rough with his large fingers. It was nice this time, though, and she found herself relaxing. She unbuttoned his shirt and ran her hands across his chest, which was firm and relatively hairless and quite unlike her husband's. Stop, she told herself. Stop comparing, stop thinking.

He pulled off her shorts and threw them onto the other bed. She had worn red satin panties, an homage to the party dress. His mouth was on them now, breathing warmth, his tongue flickering at the edges. She opened her legs wider and scooted to the edge of the bed. Maybe it was this, she thought, this one thing. Doug had never been a big fan of oral sex, either way. He was happy to put his hand to the task or to let her use hers, but the times they'd pleasured each other with their mouths were few and far between. Really, she had never thought about it much. She'd always been content with their sex life, had felt that it progressed through the type of cycle any couple experiences after years of marriage. It wasn't until Glen Hanley pressed his face up into her red dress that she felt something was missing from her life.

When he saw she had moved to the edge of the bed, he kneeled before her. Did she sense a slight hesitation? She wondered if he wanted to do something else. And because of this lingering doubt, she was unable to come or get anywhere close, so after a while she sat up and motioned for him to stand. She pulled down his plaid boxers—one of his more endearing traits, she thought—and was taken aback to find he wasn't fully aroused. In fact, she couldn't think of a time when she'd seen him so flaccid, so small.

"Sorry," he said. "I'm distracted, I guess. I had to finish a report before I left the office and it was hectic, waiting for a call from the credit bureau. Some guy took a loan under his middle name to pay off bills so he could qualify, and he thought we wouldn't find out. I had to make all kinds of phone calls, and—"

"Shh." Susan put her fingers to her lips in what she hoped was a seductive manner. The last thing she wanted to hear about was his job. She knew from experience in her marriage talk of that sort wouldn't help anything. What they needed was escape, depersonalization. She took his limp member in her hand. Clammy, curved. She fought a small wave of repulsion before she put it in her mouth.

His hand cupped her head, his fingers tangled in her hair. She kept on, in and out, swirling her tongue now and then. Slowly, it came to life. She looked up once to see Glen staring intensely out the window, not looking at her at all. But they finished, finally, and his penis rested against his thigh, brownish and sticky. She rolled away and began to put on her clothes.

"What are you doing?" he asked.

"It's a little cold in here." She walked to the thermostat and adjusted it. There was an almost imperceptible smear on the wallpaper from someone else's hand. "Why don't you open the wine now?" she asked, and she walked into the bathroom.

CHAPTER

8

Moore

Woman Starts Over

Terri feels the first swipe. The cotton swab is eight to ten inches long, dipped in an alcohol solution that will produce a slight burning sensation. So she's been told. What she really feels is a searing, a heat that spreads from forehead to cheek, from nose to chin, the swab making grand gestures now as the technician's white arm intermittently blocks the yellow glare from an overhead light. The first step, the easiest.

She's been given a long, black tube to hold. She points it towards her face and cool air streams out, acting as a balm. It's tolerable now.

"You doing all right, dear?"

Terri opens one eye. A face hovers like a low moon, craters for eyes and mouth. "Yes, it's fine."

Feet click into the room. Another face, this one right-side up. Black hair pulled back, creamy skin. The woman could be thirty or fifty.

"Hello, Mrs. Moore," she says. "I'm Dr. Chen."

"Hello," Terri says. The burning has calmed but lingers at her temples. She fights the urge to scratch her nose.

"Dr. Lee had an emergency. I'm sure Molly told you. I'll be checking on you today."

Terri shifts her hips on the table. Her knees are comfortably propped on a pillow roll, but one foot has crept out from the thin sheet.

Dr. Chen leans in, inspects Terri's face with espresso-colored eyes. "A little reddening here, and here," she says to Molly. "Looks great." She straightens, sliding one hand into the pocket of her white jacket. "Is someone waiting for you?"

"What? No." She shakes her head and adjusts the cool air away from her face. The tube makes a gentle whirring noise. "I can drive myself home."

The doctor nods and puts a hand on Terri's arm. "Molly will start the peel now. Don't be afraid. It's more intense than what you get at the spa, but it won't be bad, not really. I'll be back afterwards to have a look."

"Thank you," she says, wishing the doctor would move her hand. The thought of driving herself, being alone, suddenly makes her throat ache.

Dr. Chen leaves the room, and Molly begins to hum. She is out of sight, fiddling with something on a table she wheeled into the room when they started. Suddenly, her face appears. "Didn't you say you had two teenagers at home, dear?"

"Mm-hm."

"Couldn't they drive you?"

Terri closes her eyes. "My daughter has her license, but my son is fifteen. Anyway, they're both in Hawaii with their dad for a week."

"Oh, how nice!" She sits on the stool, which releases a soft whoosh of air. "I've never been. Have you?"

"Once," she says. "My honeymoon."

"And the kids?"

"No. Their first time." She opens her eyes. "My ex has been a few times. Since we got divorced, I mean. He's remarried now."

"What about you, dear?"

"No, I'm single." Terri looks at the ceiling. White, stark, clinical. So different from the lavish décor at Spa Energe. But she's turning forty soon and needs to up her game. Her customers expect her to look fresh and young, and she deserves to treat herself well, doesn't she? She realizes how cliché it is: spurned ex-wife gets cosmetic procedure while ex-husband takes twenty-eight-year-old new wife on a tropical trip and yet, it seemed the perfect time to recover while the kids were gone. She'd have something else to think about.

"Ok, dear," Molly says. "Here we go."

Terri closes her eyes again and clutches the black tube. It's a process, she tells herself. First, it will burn and hurt until you don't think you can take any more. But you will. She soothes herself by imagining the cool stream of air is the breeze off Maui. One of their happiest weeks. The ground-floor hotel room with its tiny balcony, swimsuits hanging on the railing to dry, tanned legs entangled in the flowered bedspread. Outside, Randy is a tiny figure on a swelling wave as the sand peaks and dips around her, a private mountain range.

She worries about Tyler, who didn't want to go on the trip with his dad and about Karly, who really did. She imagines Karly and Jamie, the new wife, laughing and shopping, huddled under an umbrella reading *Cosmo*.

It burns, really burns. She thinks of the house, what there is to do there. One day after another, one foot then the other. Something her mother used to say.

When Terri emerges from the building, her face is red and raw but shielded by the hat she was instructed to bring. Dr. Chen applied something after it was done and it took the sting out, mostly. Terri looks for her car, a pale green Audi, a new lease, and feels a wave of ease and control when she spots it. This is good, she thinks. Something new.

A Love Affair

Amber pushes against the firmness of Tyler's chest and it gives, slightly. "What are you doing?" she whispers.

"I don't know." He releases her wrists. "I thought that we, I've been thinking—"

"Mommy."

She peers around him to see Joy standing in the kitchen doorframe, holding one of the presents from her party, a Beach Barbie.

"Can you open this?" Joy asks.

"I'll get it." Tyler takes the box from her, almost roughly.

"Careful!" Joy holds up her hands, palms forward.

"Sorry," he says. "Just a minute."

Amber watches as he walks to the drawer where she keeps scissors and begins to wrestle with the packaging. There is the box, taped shut, then a plastic casing, then the twist-ties that bind Barbie to all of it. He snips and grunts, pulls and twists.

"Don't cut her hair!" Joy instructs.

"He's not," Amber says. "Now just be patient."

Joy walks over and nuzzles underneath her mother's arm. Her little white dress with yellow sunrays is rimmed at the hem with a grayish film, and there is a spot of chocolate on the bodice. She's a sunny girl, with almost-white streaks in her hair and a smattering of freckles across her nose. Unlike most children, she watches before she speaks, and she notices any small change her mother makes to their apartment. She is clever and funny and pretty in a practical way. Amber loves her a dangerous amount.

"Here she is," Tyler says. He comes forward, doll extended, and Joy breaks free to get it.

"What about the other one?" Amber asks. "Didn't you get a Ken doll too?"

"I'll open that later." Joy runs from the room, all energy.

Amber looks up and Tyler is staring at her, waiting to see.

"I should go," he says.

She notices the pattern of sun and shade made by the leaves against the window. Pockets of contrast, permuting. "Do you want a beer?" she asks.

"Sure."

She turns and opens the refrigerator. "Corona, Bud Light?"

"Bud Light?" he snorts.

"My friend Lurie brought it last weekend."

"I know Lurie," he says.

"Oh, right." She brings two Coronas to the table along with a fish-shaped bottle opener she bought in San Pedro.

"Well, she had a fight with Brandon and came over to talk about it."

They sit at the table. Her bare foot brushes his leg, warm and wooly, under the table. "Sorry," she says.

"You did that on purpose," he says, smiling.

"You wish," she replies, fighting her own smile. She takes a long drink to hide her blush. "So what about this new job?"

He leans back and his shoulders relax. She thinks, as she often has, that he doesn't seem to realize how attractive he is. In the late afternoon light, his eyes are almost completely green, no brown at all. There is a chiseled, unspoiled quality to his face—cheekbones a woman would envy, a perfect nose. But he's much less threatening sitting down, where she can see the place where his hair is mussed, where she can notice the slight tremble of his hand.

He waves the hand now, a dismissal. "Someone above me quit, that's all. I'll be the Assistant Director of IT."

"You seemed excited about it before," she says.

"I was. I am." He drinks his beer. "They seem to think I can take over for the director in a few years. You know, because it's the phone company, this vast network. Lots of opportunities to advance."

She nods. "That sounds great."

"What about you? How're things at your company?"

"I don't know. I'm not sure I can see myself there indefinitely."

He leans forward, puts his elbows on the table. "What do you want to do?"

She shakes her head. "You'll laugh."

"No, I won't."

She stands. From the top cupboard, she gets a bag of chips and makes much crinkling noise opening it.

"Well?" he says.

"I like flowers," she tells him. "I'd like to open a flower shop someday." She takes a drink from the new bottle. "I'm going to check on Joy."

Amber pauses in the hall, pressing her hands to her face. She hasn't eaten lunch, she remembers that now. With the party preparations—the cake, the games, the parents arriving from their large homes—she'd forgotten. She did have a small piece of cake but aside from that, only the beer since breakfast. She stands there in the hall, time passing. What is happening? What does he want?

Her daughter is sitting on the floor, holding the Beach Barbie and talking. She stops when Amber comes in.

"Look, Mommy," she says.

Amber perches on the side of the bed.

"She has a dress for parties, like mine only blue. And she got two swimming suits and some pants. Oh, and she has a purse, but I broke the handle already. It was only plastic." She lifts a tiny purple purse to show her.

"That's all right," Amber says. "We'll get you another one."

"She doesn't need it. She keeps her keys in her pocket, like you."

"You hungry?"

"I had two pieces of cake."

She reaches out and touches her daughter's hair. "Did you have any pizza?"

"Yeah."

The door opens and Amber jumps up.

Joy looks from her father to her mother and back again.

"I'm making sandwiches," Tyler says.

"You're both trying to feed me!" Joy says, and for some reason, finds it very funny and laughs her high-pitched, musical laugh until they're all laughing.

Amber follows Tyler to the kitchen. They eat sandwiches, finish their beers and open two more. He tells her about his parents. He feels badly because his mother is alone, but his dad is getting remarried. She tells him about her parents, who live together but separately. Her mother's bridge club and symphony tickets, her father's television.

They sit for a while on the porch, and then on Joy's pink bench. They're sillier now, more relaxed. Their legs press together and once, he finds a bread crumb in her hair. When dusk arrives, they go back into the apartment to find that Joy has fallen asleep early. Tyler lifts their daughter into her bed, and the sight of it makes something clench in Amber's abdomen. They move to the living room, where they turn on the television but don't watch. They talk about surfing and friends, about the dog Amber had when she was young, about school and sports they played and places they've gone, about siblings and grandparents, about music, about food, about time. And at some point, they walk together to Amber's bedroom, where they're careful to set an alarm so he can be gone before Joy wakes up. Only Joy comes to wake them in the middle of the night because she's hungry again. And before Amber can protest, Tyler has risen first and follows their daughter to the kitchen.

A Childhood Memory

In a bright room, on a sunny day, a newly six-year-old girl places an assortment of toys around her. There is a set of markers and a Cinderella activity book, a jewelry box inlaid with mother-of-pearl, a lanky and pert-nosed Beach Barbie.

"You need your party dress," the girl says. "And your keys."

Tongue extended, she struggles with the dress, which fits the doll snugly and has two metal snaps in the back. The shoes are difficult, and it takes her a minute to realize they have snaps, too, made to look like buttons on the tops of the shoes. She manages to get them on. She brushes Barbie's hair.

Barbie has a bed with a silk bedspread, several stylish outfits, and a purple sports car.

"You can drive yourself and go somewhere else if it's boring," the girl says. "But you have to work in the morning, don't forget."

The Ken doll peers from a box, his face impassive. The girl pushes him aside with the purple car. Barbie's hands are on the steering wheel, her smug face staring straight ahead.

"Out of the way," the girl says to Ken. "You can live in there."

CHAPTER

9

Hallowicz

Boy Meets Girl

As she turned the corner next to the gymnasium, Betsy Springer saw them: three girls arranged on the lower benches of the metal bleachers, all limbs and pastel colors. It wasn't until she got a little closer that she noticed the fourth, a boy.

"Betsy!" Thelma called. "I got my pedal pushers!" She stood up and turned around to show the pants at every angle. They were light blue in color and seemed to cut into Thelma's waist, which could be trimmer, in Betsy Springer's opinion.

The other girls, Jane and Marla, wore skirts and collared shirts. Jane's was a favorite of Betsy's—yellow with tiny birds—and Marla wore her calico skirt, too babyish and quite out of style. But Marla didn't have many outfits.

"I would've gone for the pink ones," Betsy said.

Thelma pouted. "You would, but blue's better on me."

Betsy remained several feet away and glanced at the boy sitting with his bony legs extended into the dirt.

Jane ran a hand through her blonde hair, her best feature. They all envied its shine and curl. "This is my cousin, Wilson Hallowicz."

He stood and offered his hand. "We already met. I remember."

Betsy crossed her arms over her chest, now ashamed of her own girlish blouse, her checkered skirt. You have to put in more effort, she chastised herself. All of life ahead and what will you do?

The boy was tall with wavy hair, mostly brown but shimmering here and there with red. Freckles dotted his face, mostly under his eyes and across his forehead. He had a bold way of looking at her, at all of them. "Betsy, right?" he asked.

"Yes," she answered.

"It was last January," he said. "That dance."

She shook his hand, which seemed a strange thing to do, there at the bleachers behind their high school on a summer day.

Marla moved closer. "It's still open," she whispered.

By "it" she meant the door to the Home Economics classroom, which was equipped with an oven, wide counters, and a refrigerator/freezer where they got the ice for their whiskey sours.

Marla had a bitter smell about her, and the calico skirt was wrinkled and faded in parts. "Jane brought lemons and the sugar should still be there," she said.

"What about whiskey?" Betsy asked. "I can't take any more from my dad."

"I've got it." Wilson reached over and held aloft a brown bag, crinkled around the neck of the bottle.

Jane's face gleamed, but Betsy didn't like the development. It had been the four of them, all summer, she and her friends. How would they talk about boys now, or other girls, or anything really, if *he* was there? Besides, she remembered him now. The winter formal. She had gone with Lawrence Deightly, who drove his father's Plymouth and smelled like something medicinal when he picked her up. He was a nice enough boy, and she enjoyed cracking jokes with him in Math class, but they were just friends. Jane's cousin Wilson had attended with Brenda Sykes, a cheerleader, who'd been so proud to have a date from another school, especially such a good-looking one. Between her prancing around and Jane's bragging, Betsy hadn't wanted to have anything to do with any of them.

"Why isn't Brenda here?" she asked.

Wilson looked over, his eyebrows tilted. "What? Oh, that was just a date. She's not my type."

They walked towards the building, shoes scratching and slapping against the dirt. It was a hot summer and the grass in the field was brown in sections.

Thelma hung back and walked with Wilson. "Tell us the rest of that story," she said. She poked Betsy in the shoulder with her pudgy finger. "He had us in hysterics before you got here."

"Hm," Betsy said.

"That was about it," he said. "The girl's parents found us up in the tree. Her shoe had dropped—it was black and white. What do you call them?"

"Saddle shoes," Jane said.

Wilson laughed, a contagious sound. Betsy smiled but quickly suppressed it.

"I'll never forget the sight of her father," he said, "holding that shoe and staring up through the branches. I thought I'd piss myself."

"Classy," Betsy said.

Marla opened the door to the Home Economics room and they all stepped into the cool shade. It was eerily quiet inside.

Wilson and Thelma made the drinks while the other girls sat in the back of the room in the empty desks.

Jane leaned forward and whispered: "I think my cousin likes Thelma."

Marla chewed her fingernails and looked at Betsy. In most situations, they tended to wait and see what Betsy had to say.

She couldn't think of much. She was still unsettled by his presence, still annoyed at Jane for bringing him. He was so comfortable; he'd made himself right at home amongst them. "I hope he has a good job," she said.

"Why?" Jane whispered.

She leaned forward. "Have you seen what Thelma eats on dates?"

Marla snickered. "That's terrible. And please stop talking about jobs. My mother spent most of the morning telling me about jobs."

There'd be no talk of college, not for Marla.

"Did you send the application?" Jane asked Betsy. She'd been trying to convince her to attend California Baptist

University in Riverside. Jane wanted to study books and art, but Betsy couldn't see the point of that.

"I'll probably end up taking typing," she said.

"What about nursing?" Marla asked. "That's what I'd do."

Wilson came down the aisle, Thelma trailing behind him, her face flushed. They handed each girl a drink. The cups were taken from the cupboards; they'd wash them before they left.

After the first whiskey sour, the room softened around them. They looked in the drawers and found a box of saltine crackers, which they devoured. Thelma wiped up the crumbs and scooped them into her mouth.

Wilson told another story, this one about a girl who was working at a drive-in when she saw her boyfriend in a car with another girl. He thought it was her night off. The carhop filled his tailpipe with whipped cream and wrote a disparaging message on the back window, all without his knowing.

The girls asked questions and laughed, imagining the boy and his date driving away unaware.

Betsy had warmed to Wilson. He was terribly nice and funny, although he still struck her as someone in another league. And his confidence was unnerving. He told them he worked as a roofing apprentice for his father's business. While some may wish for something more or be resentful of the obligation, Wilson actually seemed to like the work. He was content with himself in a way that none of them were. Not Jane, who wanted to study and travel, not Marla, who had few options, not even Thelma, who was easy-going and planned to attend a junior college nearby. Least of all not Betsy, who didn't have any idea what she wanted to do.

"Tell us about that boy in Milwaukee," Thelma said now.

Betsy shook her head. "No, you've already—"

Jane snorted. Her eyes were glassy from the whiskey. "But it's so funny!"

Thelma leaned over until her face was close to Wilson's.

"Betsy's like you. She always makes us laugh." His mouth tweaked into a grin. "Is that right?"

Betsy shrugged. "It's just that you girls are always drunk."

They all laughed.

"Come on," Marla said.

So Betsy told the story, about her brother's friend and the dangers of peeing outside when it's below zero. As she talked, she remembered the frigid days in Wisconsin, the sky a sullen gray and a stillness that reached to your core. Crisp leaves underfoot, gray snow creeping into your boots, hills and steam and icicles.

Wilson wiped his eyes. He touched her arm. "Let's make these alcoholics another drink."

"What time is it?" She turned her eyes towards the wall clock. Two-fifteen. Hours before dinner, which her mother expected her to make. This was a new responsibility, her mother's effort to make sure there was *something* her daughter could do. But Betsy had to be careful, had to make sure she could think straight when she arrived home.

"Got a date or something?" he asked, and the room's inhabitants seemed to inhale all at once, because of the way he said it and his unwavering gaze.

"All right, just half a glass," she said. Clumsily, she slid out from the desk.

Near the Home Economics sink, she took a knife and a lemon, her body in a state of heightened awareness as he moved near and around her. She heard the refrigerator open and ice clunk into the plastic cups. She felt his warmth as he passed by to get the sugar from the counter. And then her hand slipped, and she sliced her finger.

She gasped, and he appeared at her side.

"What happened?"he watched as a band of red appeared, as though her finger was wearing a belt.

He grabbed her by the wrist and turned on the water, which stung when it streamed over the cut.

"Ouch."

"Better than lemon juice," he said.

She watched the reddened water swirl down the drain, then she leaned against him when her eyes blurred.

"Jane!" he called.

The girls hurried to the front of the classroom, their eyes wide.

Wilson turned off the water and looked at the wound. He grabbed a towel from the counter and wrapped it around. He showed Marla how to hold it in place, tightly and keeping the hand elevated. He brought a stool for Betsy to sit on. Then he and Jane left the room.

"Where are they going?" she asked. The cut was just beginning to hurt, an ache no doubt dulled by the whiskey. But the ominous tone of the room was scaring her. "Is it that bad?"

Marla rubbed Betsy's back with her other hand. "They went to look for antiseptic, to clean it."

"Jesus," Thelma said. "I have to go." She looked back and forth between the girls.

"It's all right," Marla said. "Go."

"Sorry, Betsy. My grandparents are coming today. My dad said—"

"It's only a little cut," she said. "I'm not dying."

Thelma laughed and leaned forward. "See, you are funny. And he likes you, not me."

Jane and Wilson came back in as Thelma left. Carefully, he removed the towel from Betsy's hand. "Wow, it's really bleeding. I think you may need stitches."

"Shit," Jane said. "She can't go home like this."

Marla was washing her hands at the sink, up to the elbows. "Stitches are easy. We could do it."

"What?" Betsy stood up but Wilson kept hold of her wrist.

"It's a Home Economics room. There are needles and thread."

"You're crazy. I'm going home." She stumbled towards the door.

Jane put a hand on her shoulder. "Your mom."

And Betsy knew she was right. Something like this would push her mother over the edge. She was already so careful around her daughter, so disappointed, so tense.

Marla did the stitching while Wilson held Betsy's arm down and let her rest her face against his chest. Jane sat across the room, unable to watch. They disinfected it first and waited for the bleeding to slow. They put down towels. It took three stitches, which Betsy hardly felt, then Marla tied it off and put a bandage over the whole thing.

By the time they cleaned the room and put everything back in place, the cut had become an insistent ache. Outside, they blinked in the sunshine and tried to say goodbye.

"See you later," Jane said.

Betsy propped the wounded hand in the crook of her arm. She looked at Wilson, who stood near Jane staring at the ground. Only Marla seemed invigorated by the afternoon. She twirled on the dusty ground, her calico skirt flaring around her. Betsy remembered the evening's menu at her house: Salisbury Steak with mashed potatoes and green beans.

Jane slugged her cousin in the arm. "Let's go."

They turned in three directions and began to walk.

Betsy stopped once. "Marla!"

Her friend turned, squinted across the football field. "What?"

"You'd be a great nurse!"

Marla grinned but shook her head, and the last time Betsy looked, she was skipping as they used to do in grade school, the green all around her and her skirt making waves and swirls in the sunlight.

Reversal of Fortune

"Goddamn," Mrs. Hallowicz muttered. She had stepped into a puddle without noticing. Water seeped into her canvas sneakers above the white, rubber rim. She looked up at the Gleesons's house as if this, too, was their fault.

She shook her foot and stepped onto the porch. There was a dull humming sound inside, birdsong at her back. She rapped on the door.

Wet grass, wet pavement. Mrs. Hallowicz closed her eyes and inhaled. She remembered them—the two boys and the little girl—running through sprinklers in the front yard, their mother sipping something cold on this very porch. That Sandy Gleeson and her curls, her fleshy legs in shorts.

The door opened and Mrs. Gleeson squinted out. "Well, hello Mrs. Hallowicz." She reached up and touched her hair. "It's been some time since I've seen you." She turned the handle of the screen door. "I hope everything's—please, come inside."

"It's your daughter," Mrs. Hallowicz said.

Susan Gleeson paused, holding the screen open a few inches.

"Sandy?"

"You have another one?" the old woman asked.

"Excuse me," she said, stepping around the door and onto the porch.

In the sunlight, Mrs. Hallowicz could see she was a good-looking woman, even into middle age. "She's back living with you?"

"Should we sit?" Susan motioned to the wooden porch chairs, which Mrs. Hallowicz noticed were covered in dust.

"No. I wanted to tell you I saw her yesterday."

"Yesterday? I thought she stopped over last week, after the party." Susan looked down, her lashes disappearing against her skin.

She's quite fair, Mrs. Hallowicz thought. So is the girl, and one of the boys. The other was dark and stocky like the father.

"I'm sorry you were disturbed by the party," Susan said. "You see, my husband Doug, it was his fiftieth birthday. A big occasion, wouldn't you say?"

Mrs. Hallowicz shrugged.

"Normally, we're early birds, but I realize it may have been a little loud—"

The old woman held up her hand. "Yesterday," she said. "Your daughter was outside without any clothes on."

Susan startled, shook her head as though she hadn't heard correctly. "Sandy?"

"Yes," Mrs. Hallowicz said. "She was out there on a lawn chair without a stitch. I thought you should know."

"Well, it was her day off. She works as a pet groomer." Susan lifted her head, met the old woman's gaze. "She was living up north for a while, but now she's staying with us until she finds a place. She has always loved animals, children, even plants as you know, Mrs. Hallowicz."

"It's not proper."

Susan glanced into the house again. As though waiting for something, someone. Then she stepped to the side of the porch, her gaze following the wooden fence separating their homes. "You're talking about the back yard? She was tanning herself in *our* back yard?"

The old woman glared.

"Mrs. Hallowicz, no one would be able to see her from there. Except you."

The old woman toddled on her feet, recovered and blinked her eyes. "But is she all right, your girl?"

"Of course," Susan said. She ran a hand through her blonde hair and straightened her blouse. "She's going to be just fine."

CHAPTER

10

Hanley

A Betrayal

Janet made out the check for twenty-five hundred, even though Penny had only asked for twenty-two. The checks were patterned with photos of "National Wonders" and this one had a muted panoramic of the Grand Canyon. She hesitated on the "y" in Hanley, then let it trail off the corner of the paper. Done.

The desk in the spare bedroom had seen better days. Glen had insisted on bringing it when he came down from San Francisco, the only substantial piece of furniture he owned then. Over time, the rich brown color had faded, and Janet probably didn't give it the care it deserved. Several square cubbies were built atop the work area, which was crowned with an engraved, swirling design. She could see at this level that every little embellishment was coated with dust.

She pulled on the bottom drawer, and it came, grudgingly. One business-sized envelope and a stamp from the top, narrow drawer. As she wrote down the address, she waited for the inevitable déjà vu moment, the way her mind jumped from "Plain Township, Ohio" to Barstow, each and every time. The association seemed a natural one. In her many conversations with Penny, she'd heard much about Plain Township—its historical Main Street, the remaining farmers, the Gas n' Go where Penny operated the cash register—and Janet thought of the small-town feel of Barstow when she was growing up. Sure, both places were much changed over the decades. Housing developments expanding the borders, shopping centers replacing individual stores, paved roads and hospitals. Penny, however, had never left; she hadn't seen broader vistas, as Janet had.

In the bedroom, the afternoon light was hazy pink, a subdued shade of the rose-colored curtains Glen had thought were too girly for their shared quarters. But she'd put in all the work on the redesign, and he didn't understand how changing a single element could throw the whole thing off. She'd tried to appease him by letting him choose a slightly darker wood for the bed and dresser, and that had seemed to work. Their entire marriage sometimes seemed like a compromise, neither getting what he or she truly wanted. Maybe that's how every marriage was.

She pulled on a pair of pants and ran a brush through her wavy hair, which still seemed to be smashed on one side from a late morning nap. There was nothing to do for it now. If she wanted to get Penny's check in the mail and still have time to pick up some supplies for the fundraiser meeting, she'd have to hurry. As she hurried down the hall towards the table where she kept her keys, the telephone rang. She put the envelope down by the keys and her purse and detoured into the kitchen to answer.

"Hello?"

"Hi there, honey." A hoarse voice, a woman's. "It's me, Penny."

"You don't sound much better," Janet said, glancing at the clock. She shouldn't have answered. Sometimes it was difficult to get off the phone with her.

"No, I'm coming around. Ate some regular food today. The boss made me corn chowder."

"He didn't have to work?"

"Nooo," Penny said, drawing it out. "It's a holiday. Martin Luther. Isn't Glen's bank closed?"

Janet found her flip-flops by the back door and slipped them on. "They're staying open. Seems like some businesses are open, some are closed."

"What are you up to today?"

"Actually, I've gotta go, Penny. Some women from the PTA are coming over tonight. We're getting a fundraiser organized."

"They ask too much of you at that school. Three days a week doing the teachers' work and now they've got you making their money, too."

Janet switched the phone to her other ear. "I volunteered."

"I wish I could've helped out when my boys were in grade school. But I was always working, seemed like." She laughed. "Did I ever tell you about the time I was minding the farmer's stand, and the wheel gave out? Apples and corn all over the highway—"

"Oh, my."

"A man came by though, helped me stop traffic so I could scoop everything back up, put it back into the crates." She paused. "Sold almost everything that day anyway, and I dated that man for a couple months!"

"Penny, I'm sort of in a hurry."

"Oh, right. Okay, hon. Did I tell you Skip's football team won on Saturday? He was over the moon, that one."

"That's great."

Penny shuffled the phone around. "Um, listen, hon. Did you have a chance to send me the money? I really hate to ask again, but the doctor's office called today." She coughed. "The nurse told me how pleased they were with how it turned out. Isn't easy for an adult to have their tonsils out. She said I shouldn't get sick so much in the winter now. I appreciate you, hon, you know I do, and I'll pay you back just as soon as I get my head above water."

"I know you will," Janet said. "I'm on my way to mail the check now."

"Oh! You're a doll. Have fun at your meeting, okay?"

The dial tone sounded in Janet's ear, steady and loud. She hung up the phone, feeling annoyed and benevolent and a little unsure. It was a good thing she was doing, wasn't it? When Penny called her, those many months back, and explained who she was, Janet immediately felt sorry for her. But it was more than that. Penny was funny and warm, and soon they were talking three, four times a week. They had much in common, concerns about their children and getting older; they even watched the same television shows. After she injured her back working at a grocery store, Penny had been on disability, but it was running out. She lived with "the boss," her boyfriend Rudy, who helped with household expenses, but raising two teenage boys was difficult for a single mother. Janet couldn't imagine how she'd manage with the girls if something happened to Glen. True, she had worked before they were married, mostly office jobs, but that was so long ago now.

So she had formed a friendship with Penny. She felt certain that eventually, Glen would come around. Penny told Janet that although he hadn't been rude to her, he didn't want to keep in touch. That was fine with her, Penny said, but she thought maybe Janet should know about her in case anyone else in the family ever "got curious about their roots." Periodically, Janet felt guilty about the phone calls, but Glen hardly noticed what she did these days. The first time Penny asked for money, it was just a short loan so she could buy the football pads Skip needed for practice and the orthodontic evaluation the other needed, the younger one unluckily named Tayl. "Like tail," Penny had explained, "with a y," as though it was the most normal thing in the world.

Penny had paid back that loan, so Janet had been glad to help her out again, a month or so later. But now, this situation with the tonsils had arisen. Penny was back to work but had no insurance at the convenience store where she worked; she'd been waiting to save enough money to purchase her own. Janet felt reservations about this new loan, this larger amount and with the second still unpaid, but she felt too committed to say no. And maybe part of her was pushing the limits to see if Glen would notice.

As she reached for her keys again, the front door swung open, and she jumped.

"Oh, my God. Glen! What are you doing?" She stumbled, backed into the table. "You scared me to death."

He loomed over her, blocking the sun from the open door. "Sorry. Where are you going?"

"Errands." She turned and shoved the envelope into her purse. "Grocery store. What are you doing?"

Glen had come up behind her, was pressing himself against her and reaching around for her breasts. "Do you have some time? Just a little?" He kissed her neck.

She turned and gently pushed him. "Really? What's going on?"

He shrugged. Some of the dark hair he combed back had fallen across his forehead. "Nothing. I was thinking about you, that's all. Can't I come home for lunch?"

"You want me to make you lunch? Glen, I'm on my way to the store."

His hands went to her hips. "No, I don't really want lunch." He pulled her against his chest. "Ten minutes, come on. It's been a while."

"I know," she said. "I thought you weren't interested."

"I'm interested now."

"Well, *now* I've got things I have to do."

He backed up, shaking his head. "When, then? You're always distracted."

"We have two children!"

"Everyone has children," he said.

She set her purse down. "Fine. Let's go. Ten minutes?"

He crossed his arms over his chest and in that moment, he looked like a big, petulant child. "Oh, this is a turn-on."

Janet closed her eyes. "I'm sorry. I can't just light up when I'm in the middle of something—"

"Forget it." He turned towards the door but looked back. "I'll grab a burger. Bad idea."

"No, no it wasn't. Glen—"

He leaned over and kissed her on the forehead. "See you tonight."

And the guilt Janet felt added to what was already there, the guilt about starting a relationship with Glen's half-sister (whom he didn't care to know), the guilt about sending her money, the guilt about the bad feelings Janet was starting to have about Penny and her intentions. But she pushed it all down, looped her purse around her shoulder and finished her errands. By the time the women began to arrive in the late afternoon, her kitchen table was laid with cheese, crackers, and pastries, and the aroma of coffee permeated every room.

"Janet!" Elsie McDunnough pushed into the house with two others. "Great to see you. This is Linda Davidson, and Susan Gleeson."

Janet shook their hands. Linda was quiet and dark-haired, and Susan was curvy and blonde. They all went to the kitchen. The fundraiser was to take place in five weeks: a "Global Feast" where families would bring ethnic dishes, and everyone could sample each other's cuisine. Families would pay to eat at the potluck, and the funds would be used for the school's art and music program. Janet was usually skilled at focusing a meeting, at organizing forces and talents. But the conversation kept getting diverted by Susan, who talked a lot about the real estate program she'd just started, and her kids, two of whom were older and therefore, having experiences the other women would learn about "someday." Only her youngest, a girl, was still in grade school.

Distracted by the day's events, Janet's mind wandered throughout the meeting. She had tried to call Glen when she got back from the store, but he hadn't answered his office line. Maybe he was right. She had felt distracted lately, unsettled. There was so much about her life that she loved. The girls were wonderful—bold, bright Kizzy and Lurie, Janet's little helper. She loved their house and where they lived. Glen was a good father and provider. And yes, maybe things had slowed down in the bedroom but wasn't that normal? She'd be forty soon and although she really didn't think about it much, maybe this upcoming birthday *was* bothering her. She'd gotten very involved at the school, both volunteering in the classroom and serving on the PTA, and she met friends once in a while for lunch or a movie. There were occasional parties, and they'd taken some lovely family vacations. And yet, still, sometimes she felt a mild panic. She rarely thought about sex, that much was true.

She was standing at the kitchen counter, making a second pot of coffee for the women, when the back door opened and she heard murmurs, and the sound of shuffling feet. She turned to see Glen standing in the kitchen and looking very surprised, with a bouquet of pink and purple flowers in his hand. And for a moment, he was the young man she'd met in San Francisco: the broad shoulders, the dimpled chin.

"Oh, this is my husband," Janet said. She introduced everyone and took the flowers, which seemed to impress the women and embarrass Glen. He exchanged a few pleasantries and quickly made an exit. His love, thwarted again.

Janet looked at the clock, willing the women to leave. The girls were at a friend's house, and the mother would be dropping them at any moment. Janet wanted her dinner, she wanted to be alone, she didn't know what she wanted. And her indecision was ruining everything, she felt, and she had no idea how to turn back.

CHAPTER

11

Moore

Couple Starts a Family

"Joy!" Terri sets the plastic-handled Chipmunks spoon next to the bowl of cereal. Her granddaughter is almost nine but still wants to use it whenever she stays over. They'd gotten the silverware set at Disneyland when Joy was maybe four or five. Most girls that age would have chosen one of the princesses.

She skips down the hall, a tornado of life, touching the walls as she goes along. "Where are they today?"

Terri looks up, running the ship's itinerary through her mind. Day three. "They should be pulling into Cabo San Lucas," she says.

"What's the other one?"

"Puerto Vallarta."

Joy bends one of her skinny, down-covered legs, like a colt, and sits down.

"Feet under the table," Terri says.

She complies, leans forward, and starts on the cereal.

There is much crunching and slurping, but Terri doesn't correct her as she may have done with her own children, many years before. She is always noticing the ways grandparenting and parenting differ; table manners fall into the "not my problem" category. It's a relief, actually. When you're a parent, everything seems to be your problem. The only reason she had insisted on a proper sitting position was because Joy had knocked yesterday's bowl onto the carpet with her knee.

Joy wipes the back of her hand across her mouth. She is a pretty girl, with light hair and Tyler's green, brown-speckled eyes. She seems to take after his physique as well, the long legs and high, squared shoulders. "What are we doing today?" she asks, her mouth full of cereal.

Terri holds the mug of herbal tea in her hands. It is still damp outside, foggy and dense. June gloom, they always call it, but it's July now. "We're going to visit your grandpa today," she says. "He needs help with something."

They'd had the wedding in Randy's backyard, next to the pool and surrounded by rose bushes. Jamie had insisted on tearing up the existing landscaping when they bought the house, which was large and showy and surprisingly, further away from the beach than Randy had ever lived. The large, grassy area was outlined by roses in every hue, something Jamie had always wanted. Along with a big house and somebody else's husband, Terri thinks. But the wedding *had* been lovely. Amber wore an off-the-shoulder gown with no train, white blooms in a crown across her head. Tyler was beaming, teeth on display all day, handsome and angular in his navy blue suit. They still seemed so young and yet there was Joy, proof of their past, strewing blooms across the manicured lawn. Terri sat in the front row, Randy on one side and Karly on the other. She hated to admit it, but her ex-husband looked fabulous. His tanned skin against the white shirt collar, his athletic body evident beneath fitted clothing. She noticed some strain in his face; his recent divorce and financial problems had caused a slight weight loss. But he seemed to be over the worst of it.

Joy lifts the bowl to her mouth and finishes the rest of the milk. "Are we helping Grandpa Randy move?"

"No," Terri says. "He won't be moving for a few more weeks. He wants us to get some things down from a closet, though. It's hard for him with his leg in the cast. And he wants to see you, of course."

"When are we leaving?"

She finishes her tea and slaps her palms on the table. "Now. You ready?"

Randy and Jamie's house is in a gated community and it feels strange for Terri to give her own last name to the security guard. She wonders if Jamie will keep it or go back to her maiden name. She kept the "Moore," but she and Randy had children together. Jamie doesn't have any, an inequity Terri secretly enjoys.

The house is beige with dark brown trim, with a pretentious wooden carriage-style garage door and multi-colored pavers winding down to the street. People try to make these cookie-cutter homes look like something from a country estate, Terri thinks, and yet they are crammed in, one on top of the other. Randy gave up his homey bungalow near the beach, and near the home they had shared, for this.

"Let me," Joy says at the door.

Terri lifts her so she can reach the knocker, a brass lion's head. They hear a door shut and the slow squeaking of Randy's crutch along the tile floor. When he opens the door, his eyes—bright, questioning—go first to Terri, then down to take in their granddaughter.

"There's my girl." He braces himself for her hug, which is polite and brief. "Come in, please."

Along the entryway, boxes are stacked, some open, some sealed shut with tape. Joy hops from one to the next, pulling back the cardboard flaps, peeking inside. As they turn the corner into the sun-drenched family room, Terri notices a table. "Are you expecting company?" she asks.

"Donuts!" Joy yells, hurrying over.

"Honey, I'm not sure Grandpa Randy wants you to have those."

He jabs his crutch into the tile and looks at her. "This is for you," he says. "Help yourself."

There is coffee and hazelnut creamer (Terri's favorite), a container of cut fruit, donuts and croissants. Joy pulls back a chair from the table and reaches across for a donut.

Terri doesn't have the heart to tell him they've already eaten, so she takes a few chunks of cantaloupe and a croissant. They linger at the table, quietly eating.

Joy finishes her donut and jumps up. "Can I go in the pool? Grandma Terri has my swimsuit in her purse—"

"I said that—"

"—she said I had to ask you first and maybe your pool wouldn't be cleaned up anymore because it costs a lot of money, and you have to move."

Randy keeps his eyes on Joy. "The pool is in perfect shape. If it's all right with your grandma, you can hop in whenever you want."

They move to the patio, where a set of padded furniture is arranged under the awning. From there, they can keep an eye on her. Joy is a seasoned swimmer, having grown up with swim lessons and endless summer pool parties.

"How's your leg?" Terri asks, sipping at her coffee.

Randy has propped the injured limb onto an ottoman and is rubbing his thigh above the cast. "Still sore once in a while, but better." He puts his hands behind his head and leans back. "You love this, don't you?"

She raises her eyebrows. "What?"

"You think a fifty-year-old man deserves to break his fibula if he's foolish enough to drive a dune buggy with his foolish friends."

"Fifty-four," she says.

"I'll stick to surfing from now on," he says. "When can I take Joy out?"

"That would be up to her mother," Terri says. "And Tyler."

Joy calls to them from the pool, insisting they watch her jump from the diving board. She leaps up and spreads her limbs like a starfish before falling into the water.

"Any word from the honeymoon?" Randy asks.

"They called from Long Beach, but I'm not sure about cell phone reception out at sea." She leans forward and puts her coffee mug onto a mosaic-inlaid table. "I told them not to worry."

"They'll have a great time," he says. "They really seem to be in love. She's a good girl, that Amber. I've never seen Tyler so happy."

Tears mist Terri's eyes. "I know."

"Remember our honeymoon? Those long afternoons and the little balcony where you liked to sit."

"Don't." Terri takes off her sunglasses and wipes at her eyes. "We were talking about Tyler, and I want to thank you again for pitching in for the cruise. Amber's parents were so kind, taking care of the wedding after all they've done, and I'm glad you and I could do this for them." She glanced at the pool, where Joy was floating on her back in the deep end. "Life gets so busy and goes so fast. They won't have time for many vacations for a while. I'm so proud of them. Tyler's doing well at his job. You know, he's in line for another promotion, and Amber's looking around for a store to start her flower business. I think they'd like to try for another child, too."

"Your eyes," Randy says. "They're different."

Terri looks at him, makes an exasperated sound, and puts her sunglasses back on. "No, they're not." She'd had an eyelift before the wedding, a minor thing really, and he hadn't noticed then.

"You look great, Terri, that's all I meant."

She puts her feet up next to his on the ottoman. "Thank you. When she's done swimming, we'll help you with the stuff in the closet."

He watches her across the sunny space, his eyes crinkling in the corners as they've always done. "I'll be glad to get out of this behemoth."

"Be—, what?"

"It's my new word. It means something gigantic. Seems to fit this place, don't you think? I'm going to enjoy scaling down. They have everything I need at the Villas. I'll have two bedrooms, a fitness room, a pool."

"Where is Jamie living?" Terri asks.

"She moved in with her sister until we sell this place. The behemoth. Then she'll probably buy a condo or something." He smiles and says it again, "Behemoth."

She chuckles. "You're strange."

Joy comes from the pool, dripping and grinning. "I need a drink of water, Grandpa Randy. My mom tells me never to drink the chloride water."

"She's right about that," Terri says. "Chlorine."

Randy starts to struggle, inching forward on his chair and reaching for his crutch.

"I can get it," she says.

"No, I've gotta keep moving. It's better for the leg."

And Terri watches his effort, the determination causing a vein to bulge at the side of his temple, his inhalations as he pushes up and balances. It reminds her of when he installed the brick wall enclosing their backyard, after they moved to the little stucco house. He hadn't really known what he was doing, but he spent three weekends doing it. Once, he had to tear down a whole section that was crooked. The bricks still stood at her house, straight if a little faded by time.

She takes Joy's towel, squeezes her long hair with it, and wraps it around the girl's narrow shoulders.

"You should move in here, Grandma Terri." Joy says, clutching the towel near her neck. "It's so big and the pool is great!"

Terri looks over, but Randy has moved into the kitchen and is filling a glass at the tap. "I have my own house, sweetie. Grandpa Randy needs to live by himself for a while."

Joy shrugs, her youthful mind already onto other things. At the table, she grabs another donut and glances back to see if her grandmother will say anything.

Not my problem, Terri thinks. She steps over the threshold into the echoing expanse of the huge house, which is still cold despite the sun blazing outside. What a behemoth, she thinks, what a waste. She helps herself to another croissant and watches Joy drink the water in breathless, impatient gulps.

Girl Grows Up

Sherelle Anderson taps the pen against the side of her head, reading the evening's reports. Six infants in the nursery currently, a light load. Mrs. Gutierrez is still in labor but should be delivering shortly. Tina signed out at six o'clock, but there is only white paper where Karly Moore should have written her notes. She is one of the newer nurses, eager but unseasoned, and a source of exasperation for Sherelle Anderson, who has been working at Long Beach Memorial for twenty-two years. She'd come up the system like these new girls, working all the crappy shifts and dealing with a succession of head nurses over the years. And she was a single mother to boot, raising three boys while keeping her job, her sanity, her house.

She starts down the hall, thinking of her sons, all tall and musky-smelling now, grown men with respect and self-respect, like she taught them. She has reasons to be proud, doesn't she? These babies at the hospital, sometimes born to intact families, sometimes entering an unraveling situation or the flimsiest of circumstances—she never judges. A baby is a baby is a baby, and every mother deserves care and respect. Every person equal. This is the basic belief she thinks makes her a good nurse and a well-liked supervisor. And yet, these new nurses, these silly, over-anxious girls, they can drive her crazy.

Sherelle Anderson presses the code into the nursery door and enters quietly. In the corner, one baby has freed her legs from the swaddling blanket, and she goes there first, to tuck her back in. And it isn't until Sherelle straightens and turns that she sees Karly Moore, in another corner, fast asleep in the gliding chair with an infant pressed against her chest. The little boy born yesterday afternoon to the young mother who refuses to nurse. She's scared and tired and wanted to sleep instead. Her mother and aunts gathered around, pecking and cajoling, but she couldn't be convinced. As though he sensed the uncertainty of his situation, the baby had been particularly fussy, even after a formula feeding.

Sherelle Anderson wonders how much of Karly's shift has been taken up caring for him. She shakes her head, a smile spreading across her face. A ray of sunshine, just like that. Carefully, she weaves through the bassinets, places one hand on the baby's back and one on Karly's shoulder, and gently rouses the young nurse from sleep.

CHAPTER

12

Hallowicz

Family Survives Disaster

In most cases, Wilson Hallowicz was a man of his word. He directed his business with an iron fist and a clear conscience, following basic tenets that seemed to him common sense. Do what you mean and mean what you say. Nothing worth having comes easy. The harder you work, the luckier you get. He supposed these were guidelines he had learned by osmosis from his father, working side by side with the man for almost twenty years. His father had built the roofing company from the ground up. An apt metaphor for a roofing company, Wilson always thought. He couldn't think of a day in his life when his father didn't accomplish *something*; it just didn't happen. The elder Hallowicz treated customers and employees fairly, conducted an honest business, and expected the same from others. In his time away from work, he read newspapers and watched the news. He kept his house in working order.

Wilson had taken over the business a few years back, but his father stayed on part-time. He would have thought his father had many more years of work in him, but the older man insisted he was nearing retirement. Wilson thought he merely wanted to make sure his son could do the job. So he ran the place as his father always had; it came naturally. At home, sometimes things were different. Today, for example, Wilson found himself in the distressing position of sneaking around his own house, having told his wife that he wanted a nap when really he wanted the opposite. He would stay alert. They could sleep through the day, so to speak, if they wanted. They could pretend, but he would not.

He pulled aside the blinds and peered to the right side of the front yard, where his wife was planting rows of bulbs. The tiny plants had arrived that morning, dropped off by the nursery she'd been frequenting for years. He'd almost tripped on them when he finally went out for the paper. Yellow-bloomed plants in disposable green containers were lined up next to similar seedlings with purple flowers, then a row of white that reminded him of popcorn. Betsy had been out all morning, planning the order and preparing to plant. When Wilson saw the spade appear, saw the first bit of earth cracked and scooped out, that's when he came inside. She'd be busy for some time.

He hadn't seen Robbie most of the morning. After breakfast, the thirteen-year-old had headed out on his bicycle to meet up with friends. Wilson worried they'd make trouble at the abandoned warehouse again, but Robbie had promised they were done with that. He really was a good kid most of the time. Wilson couldn't always tolerate his mood swings, but Betsy seemed more patient with them, and Robbie was a hard worker. That was the most important thing.

Memories make the heart grow fonder, he thought. Or was it absence? Either way, it would do. He pulled the small chair away from his wife's vanity, opened the closet, and used the chair to climb up and reach the top shelf. There in the back, behind a plastic box of 8mm reels (*that* he couldn't do), was a large shoebox. Work boots, which got him thinking about his days as an apprentice under his father. The view from a site, a landscape of rooftops broken up by streets and in the distance, hills. The future stretched out before him.

Carefully, he stepped down from the chair and walked to the bed. Soon, he had all the items spread out: photos, a clay figurine, a blue ribbon for Art, notes scribbled in crayon. The intangibles flooded back. Soft hands on the back of his neck. Picking the boy up by his overalls as he giggled and kicked his feet. The squeaky voice, the endless questions. Wilson let the tremors come when they would, pausing now and then to wipe his eyes with a handkerchief. Happy birthday, Stevie. How do we go on without you? How do we not?

In time, a sharp rapping jarred him from his memories. Wilson left everything out for her to see and went to the door.

Robbie kicked his heels against the dry earth and watched as miniature clouds of dust rose. In his hand, a few jagged stones, which he shifted and tossed. He leaned back against the fence.

Heidi Baxter, Heidi Baxter, Heidi Baxter. If he said her name too many times, it began to sound strange, foreign. He thought about the way she grabbed Theo's arm when she laughed. As if anything he said was *that* funny.

In the corner of the yard, the turtle finally came out from under his wooden house. Robbie vaguely remembered building the structure with his dad. They went to the lumber yard and Robbie rode in the back of the roofing company truck. Now, they had a different truck, a newer one.

He put his fingers into a jagged tear at the corner of his jeans. His new jeans, and his mom would give him hell over that when she saw it. He's lucky he didn't get killed, he thought, then something rose in him to think it. None of them should be hanging out at the warehouse. They'd already been caught once, and his parents hadn't been happy with that phone call. But it was a big building and sort of exciting to break in and besides, it's not like the place was locked up well. They just parked their bicycles in the back, climbed onto some old barrels, and went right through an open window.

Six kids had been there today, two girls. Heidi had long brown hair parted down the middle and long legs. Robbie had watched her climb onto the barrels and looked over to see all the boys doing the same. But she liked Theo, that much was obvious.

Robbie threw one of the rocks towards the house, where it bounced under the kitchen window and vanished into a bush. He waited for his mom to appear in the window, but she didn't. Maybe she was still out in the front yard, walking around in those stupid yellow boots and broad hat. Embarrassing.

Charlie had been the first to make the climb. Up a supporting wooden beam, where huge nails had been inserted for steps, onto the iron rafters stretching from one side of the warehouse to the other. Charlie was wiry and athletic. He played basketball and could jump three feet off the ground. Once he made it up, he walked around, tightrope-style, and hollered down to them, showing off. Robbie watched Heidi's upturned face, her wide grin and shining eyes, and before he knew what he was doing, he said, "I'm next."

What Charlie had in dexterity, Robbie had in strength. He was a good runner and could outlast most, but he wasn't balanced. His long limbs often seemed out of his control and worse yet, he had a fear of heights.

"Let's see it, Hallowicz." Theo stood next to Heidi, his arms crossed over his chest. He was Robbie's good friend, but it didn't feel like it at that moment.

And so Robbie had clambered up, first gripping the beam and finding the nails for steps, inwardly panicking every moment that his foot would slip, or a nail would dislodge, then onto the rafters where he shakily held on and finally, stood. He was coated in sweat by then, his heart pounding. He had torn his jeans on one of the nails. Charlie started to come towards him on the high beam and Robbie waved him off. And when he finally felt secure and looked down to see how his feat had been received, he saw that the remaining four were joking amongst themselves, not watching at all. And it occurred to him how selfish he was, how thoughtless to put himself in jeopardy, and for what? The rafters were really high and what if he were to fall, what then? Easy for him to take life for granted. The rest of them had no idea.

The turtle made his way toward the carrot in the center of the pen. His brown, bumpy legs seemed to move, one at a time, as though it were quicksand and not plain dirt. Every so often, he'd stop altogether and raise his head.

"Stupid turtle," Robbie said. Slowly, he separated one stone from the rest and raised his arm. The turtle's wooden home was surrounded by chicken wire, also installed years ago. Robbie grunted and released the stone, which hit the thin wire instead of going through. It ricocheted and fell, having no effect on the turtle.

A sliding sound, metallic. The kitchen window. His mother called, "Robbie, you stop bothering that turtle! Do you hear me? Robbie?" And something about her voice made him get up and walk around the house where he could see her. She leaned over the sink, her face close to the opening. Was she crying? For a few moments, they stood there in the afternoon light, looking at each other through the screen. Then she vanished into the house.

"Damn," Robbie said, kicking again at the dirt.

"Goddamn," Mrs. Hallowicz said under her breath. "Ah, you poor thing." Gently, she removed one stem from the seedling she held in her hand. It had been damaged when she'd removed the plant from its disposable container. She bent down and nestled the clump of soil and roots into the hole she'd dug for it, then she smoothed the dirt down around the plant and patted it. Straightening up, she looked down at her work.

She'd arranged the flowers in a layered design: yellow blossoms around the edges of the oval section next to the front door, a line of purple inside that, then white in the middle. Pleased with her work, she pulled off her gloves and set them on the bottom step leading to the porch. The day had turned very warm, too warm for May. She remembered that time, the party when they had to bring all the kids into the house, their muddy shoes and the sodden cake.

Mrs. Hallowicz reached up and took off her hat. She noticed that Robbie's bicycle was thrown down in the narrow dirt area between the house and the fence. He must have returned at some point, maybe when she'd gone in for a drink of water. Looking over the fence, she made a mental note to stop by and see Mr. Rivera next door. His wife had been gone for six months by then; he was in his eighties and doing poorly. Mrs. Hallowicz had noticed more visitors lately. It wasn't her nature to be particularly neighborly, but she felt in this case, with the poor man all alone, she could at least take some food.

Wilson had gone in for a nap, which wasn't like him. She worried for a moment whether he was coming down with something. She could always depend on him, on his strength. He rarely missed work, and she could count on one hand the times he'd been ill since they'd married fourteen years ago. Lately, he'd been working long hours. When his father stepped down as president of the roofing company and signed everything over to them, she'd been happy for the security the change ensured but wary of the responsibility, too. And sure enough, Wilson started spending more and more time there. Many nights, she and Robbie ate dinner alone, and she'd wrap Wilson's plate in foil for later. She missed watching the news with him in the evenings, hearing his opinions. She missed having his help with Robbie, who was thirteen and usually uncommunicative and moody. Wilson was always an upbeat presence in the house, whistling and joking, always something to talk about. Left to their own devices, she and Robbie could practically live in silence.

The door clicked into place, and Mrs. Hallowicz walked down the hallway. She tread lightly, in case Wilson was still resting. She started to unbutton the long-sleeved shirt she'd been wearing since morning. A tank top would be better for the afternoon. The knob of their bedroom door didn't turn and surprised, she knocked lightly. She had her shirt completely unbuttoned by the time Wilson opened the door.

"Did I wake you?" she asked, pushing by him. She removed her shirt and threw it onto one of the bedposts. Then, she saw. Turning to him, her thick-strapped bra cutting into her shoulders, her face drained, her mouth open. "No," she said. "No. What do you think—" She stopped herself, snatched the shirt and almost ran out of the room.

In the kitchen, she stood next to the sink, shaking. She heard something strike the side of the house. Robbie. What was he doing? How could he? She forced herself to drink a glass of tap water, to slow her breathing. Another small pinging noise and she knew. Leaning over, she slid the kitchen window open. Anger burbled up, too much, too encompassing. It took all her energy not to scream at him, to make him explain, and then she hated herself for blaming him, a little boy, the boy she had left. Robbie came forward from the yard and looked at her. He sees, Mrs. Hallowicz thought. He knows.

CHAPTER

13

Hanley

A Love Story

The pains began at nine o'clock. Kizzy had just finished a very large glass of Chardonnay and the sixth episode of a DVD set Lurie had loaned her. Each one-hour installment included a murder and some very attractive people attempting to solve it. Putting together the clues was like a puzzle, trying to guess what had happened. Except Kizzy never could.

She rose from the sofa, empty glass in hand, and the first, stabbing pain sliced through her abdomen. "Oh," she said. And in that short-lived, surprising moment, her perspective broadened: the empty apartment, the black night outside, the distance and time it would take to reach her mother.

The pain subsided and Kizzy took a deep breath. What would Mahsa say if she knew that Kizzy had summoned her mother in this moment of need? Ridiculous to compare, she thought. Her mother, living alone. They had depended on each other for some time, that was all. Her mother had access to Kizzy's accounts; she knew her insurance information. Practicalities.

In the kitchen, she rinsed her glass and when she leaned over to put it into the dishwasher, another pain exploded below her waistline. This time it faded but persisted. Kizzy hobbled to the table, thinking as she did about her grandfather in Barstow, the accident that ruined his leg. He had a cane but hated using it. Every time Kizzy visited with her mother, he spent a good portion of the day in his chair, barking orders to her grandmother and watching endless golf tournaments. Her mother said he'd never watched the sport when she was growing up. You can count on it, her grandfather explained, because it's always sunny somewhere.

Kizzy lowered herself onto a chair. She pressed her hand against her side. They had argued the night before, she and Mahsa. That stupid wedding. Mahsa's insecurities. It wasn't what she thought, not at all. Kizzy just wanted to meet her family some other time. She didn't want to cause a scene at the brother's wedding, didn't want people talking or judging or trying too hard. And she didn't know what Mahsa expected. Slow dances? Hand holding? They'd only been public in very comfortable spaces, and it was all too much to think about. Mahsa said she was being ridiculous, that her family knew who *she* was, and that Kizzy was the only one with a problem.

"And while we're at it," she had said, "why haven't I met *your* mother? I know Lurie's in Denver but your mother, she lives so close!"

They were standing in the kitchen, Mahsa at the entry, headed out, Kizzy holding a half-peeled banana like a prop from a sitcom. It was something she hated, how she often felt foolish around Mahsa, who was tall and gorgeous and always put-together. Even then, in her sleek pajama bottoms and tank top scrunched to allow a peek of her navel, her hair glossed back and tucked behind each ear, Mahsa looked like a magazine spread: Casual Morning Look.

Kizzy set down the banana. "You know what happened. My dad. I'm not sure she could handle it."

"It's been six years since he died," she said. "And usually, they already know."

"She doesn't," Kizzy said. "Also, the cultural stuff, I wouldn't know what to do."

Mahsa crossed her arms. "You eat Persian food. You talk to people. You know we're not ultra-Persian. My brother's marrying a Protestant from Riverside!"

Kizzy shoved a bagel into the toaster, pressed the lever down. "Your family won't like me. You're a doctor, and I'm an accountant."

"You're right. They hate accountants."

"I'm older!"

"Three years!" Mahsa pulled her tank top down, covering her stomach, which Kizzy knew to be covered with a fine layer of shimmering hair that could only be seen up close. "You're making excuses," Mahsa said. "You're ashamed."

"No, I'm realistic."

"What about *your* mother? Do you think she'll like me?" She stepped forward, arms extended. "I'm dark-skinned, foreign. Right? I'm not a blonde financial planner like your sister's husband."

"She doesn't care about skin color or jobs or—"

Kizzy grabbed the toasted bagel and when she realized how hot it was, threw it onto the counter.

"Exactly," Mahsa said. "You're underestimating her and maybe you're overestimating me. I'm not sure how much longer I can wait."

Kizzy watched her leave the kitchen, the plump curves of her under the silky pajamas, long, dark hair brushing her shoulder blades. Mahsa always smelled good—citrus, powder, even her sweat. Kizzy chewed on the bagel and retrieved the banana, now bruised in the middle, but she forced herself to eat it anyway. She didn't hear from Mahsa for the rest of the day. They'd been spending most nights at Kizzy's lately, but there was no word from her that night and now another day had passed, another evening.

The next round of pain took her breath away. The hairs rose on the back of her neck. She imagined Mahsa at her office, talking to her patients in that musical voice, reassuring and explaining. She let herself imagine Mahsa was thinking about her between appointments, not the argument but when they were good. The conversations, the comfort, the heights. Clutching her side, Kizzy picked up the telephone and pressed the familiar numbers.

When she woke up, the sun was shearing the hospital room with blades of white. She blinked and blinked, her eyes slowly adjusting. She felt a pressure on her hand and looked over. There, in the whiteness, her mother waited.

"Hello, sleepy head."

"Mom."

"It's all over, Kizzy." She reached over and pushed a strand of hair from her face. "Everything went great, no problems at all."

"Are you sure?"

Her mother's eyes were still lively and vivid, her figure trim and almost girlish. None of Kizzy's friends ever believed she was sixty years old. "I'm completely sure," she said. "You are now appendix-free. And no one has ever missed their appendix, believe me. Funny, isn't it, that we still have one?"

"I don't."

"True." She released Kizzy's hand and patted her leg. "Lurie sends her love. And Brandon. And the kids."

"You shouldn't have worried her," she said.

"She's your sister."

A nurse walked in. Young, blonde. "We're awake?"

"We are," her mother said.

She nodded at Kizzy then turned. "Janet, can I ask you to step out of the room for a moment?"

Janet. Kizzy felt like the last person to arrive at a party.

Her mother smiled strangely, glanced at the door. "Yes, but there's someone else waiting to see you."

Kizzy looked toward the hallway. "Who?"

"Mahsa's here. She's been here the whole time, but she went down for a soda." She pressed Kizzy's hand again. "She's been worried."

The nurse pulled a pair of rubber gloves from her pocket and looked expectantly at Janet.

"Yes, I'll be right back. I'll find her."

Kizzy closed her eyes. Temperature, blood pressure, a jotting down of numbers on a page the nurse kept from her gaze. Clear liquid dripping from a translucent sac. Tape pulling at the loose skin on the top of her hand. These small stimuli, this bed with its crisp sheets and elevated view. Green on the small screen and blue through a distant window. Sounds from the hallway, from the machine keeping time and track nearby.

"There you are," Mahsa said. Unafraid, she smiled at the nurse and strode into the room. A can of Diet Pepsi in one hand, the other pulling Kizzy's mother along. Together, they stood at the side of the bed.

"Are you okay?" Janet asked. Her eyelids drooped slightly. Kizzy wondered how long she'd been watching over her.

"They're just checking my vitals," she said. "Apparently, I have some."

"I didn't know you were awake," Mahsa said. "Did you want something? They have Coke, 7-Up—"

"No, no. I'm sure it's an all-inclusive resort." She looked away. "Save your money."

Janet put her hand on Kizzy's shin and squeezed. "I'm going home now."

"What, why?"

"I left some shirts in the dryer and I'm getting hungry for dinner. Let Mahsa get something for you. I doubt the food here is very good." She straightened up and began digging around in her purse. "There's a Coco's across the street, also an Albertson's. They have a decent salad bar."

"Mom."

"Kizzy, the nurse said everything was one hundred percent normal. They do this every day, just about. You'll go home tomorrow morning, and I'll see you then. In the meantime, let her get you something." She scooted around Mahsa, leaned over, and hugged Kizzy. Her face was very close and the smell of her shampoo—lemon, nutty—made Kizzy's eyes water.

"I love you," Janet whispered. "You're going to be fine."

Kizzy patted her mother's back, felt her compactness, the ballast of her shoulder blades. Through her hair, she saw Mahsa waiting.

"Let her, Kizzy," Janet whispered. "Just let her."

Couple Starts a Family

Lurie stared out the window, watching the snow swirl in flurries onto the tarmac. Nearby, two little girls were coloring with crayons on the dirty airport carpet, their little legs splayed into Vs, their parents collapsed against each other on the chairs above them. The plane was already two hours past departure time.

A bottle of Aquafina appeared, an arm clothed in black. She looked up as Brandon squeezed in next to her, still holding the bottle inches from her face.

She snatched the water and nestled it between her thighs. There was nowhere else to put it, unless she wanted to lay it sideways on the shelf of her stomach. She'd have to wriggle and stretch to get her purse from the floor.

"I talked to her again," Brandon said.

"The nice one or the mean one?" Lurie asked.

"Nice. She thinks we'll board within the hour." He ran a hand through his blonde hair, then rested it on her neck. "How're you holding up?"

"Fine." She turned away, remembering the drive to the airport, the box of tissues he'd been thoughtful enough to grab from the bathroom. She hadn't needed them for most of the thirty-five-minute drive, not until she could see Denver International Airport, the succession of white peaks that brought to mind a circus tent, and then the thought that all of it could be a farce, some kind of grotesque performance, that danger could truly be contained, controlled, tamed like a lion—this is what made the tears come. She had always hated circuses.

"Want something to eat?" Brandon asked now.

She wiped at the side of her eyes. "No thanks." She thought of the baby, their boy. The ultrasound two days ago, their exuberant news followed so quickly by the phone call. The pregnancy had been a rollercoaster of emotions and in the grand scheme, this past tragedy juxtaposed with some little ray of happiness—well, this too seemed to be just what she deserved. Selfish, selfish, she reminded herself. And probably ghastly, too, thinking of her father's death in terms of how it affected her pregnancy, her life. And yet this is exactly what she hasn't been able to stop, not from the first moment they found out they'd be having a baby. These thoughts, these horrible thoughts. She was sure something would happen, that it would never work out. Because of what she'd done, what they'd done. That first pregnancy, which seemed so long ago. She could, at times, tell herself it was only a procedure, a necessary medical intervention from her youth. What would the other choice have been, really? She was still in school; Brandon was busy "deciding whether he wanted a commitment" at that point in his life. Screwing that girl was what he was really busy doing, but didn't Lurie have her dalliances, too? She wondered about her body; was it healthy enough to grow another life or had it been damaged? Sometimes she imagined a scarred, echoing part of her womb, traumatizing the new baby, altering his growth. All of it quite insane, but the thoughts were there. She didn't deserve another chance, did she? And now there was the snow and the delay and oh, God—there was her father.

"We may have to consider Glen or Albert for names now," she said, her voice breaking.

Brandon nodded, chewed his gum in the crackling way she hated. He had liked her father. They golfed together whenever they visited California, and they talked business. Both men worked with money, with numbers. For a few years, Brandon had been giving her father some basic financial planning advice. Lurie wondered now if he'd had some sort of premonition about dying.

The overhead speaker broke the silence. They were preparing the plane now, the woman said. The storm was clearing. On the ground, the little girls were putting their crayons away, carefully, neatly. They were quiet girls, low maintenance. Not at all how she remembered she and Kizzy to be. No wonder he strayed, she thought. Did any of us give him any notice at all?

"Will your aunts be there?" Brandon asked. "They're a trip."

Lurie's aunts, Dina and Cheryl, both still lived in northern California. Dina was a high school teacher and had never married. Cheryl and her husband ran a dog kennel and always had at least four of five dogs of their own.

"I'm sure they will be." Lurie watched as an elderly man pulled his wife from a chair. "I wonder if my grandfather is still alive."

"Nobody ever heard from him?"

She shook her head. Once she overheard her mother telling some women in the kitchen that Glen's father had "disappeared from the face of the earth." Lurie was about seven or eight at the time and she remembered thinking about earthquakes, the way they cause cracks in the ground. Maybe they had studied it in school, too, around that time. At any rate, she always imagined her grandfather standing in a field, or on a street, or near his own house, the earth shaking and opening up below him. A fault line. His fault, another association she always made.

The baby kicked and squirmed, and Lurie's breath caught. And she thought again about that first pregnancy, the decision and the aftermath. She reached over and held Brandon's hand as the thoughts came again, round and round in their cruel, circular logic, all of it ending where it began. She wondered if she'd ever be able to look at the baby, their son, without having it happen.

Outside, the snow had stopped. Busy, lighted vehicles spun around the wet expanse, cleaning and clearing. They'd be able to make it to California before morning after all. It's one good thing, Lurie thought, and she pressed her other hand against her stomach to let the boy know she was still there.

CHAPTER

14

Moore

A Love Story

Terri Moore lifts her foot out of the shoe and wiggles her toes. Glancing back, she sees the beginning of a blister in the deep grooves of skin above her heel. A tall woman passes by; they do a quick-footed do-si-do in the small corridor. Here, it's much quieter than in the main part of the restaurant, and Terri's friends can't see her from the table.

She flips open her cell phone and holds down the 3 button. She's allowed ten direct dial numbers, and she bumped her own mother down to the 8 position for him. 1 is home; 2 is work. Ringing on her phone sounds more like a blare, and she holds it away from her ear.

"Hello?"

She turns toward the wall, presses the cell phone closer. "Hi, where are you?"

"I fell asleep," he says.

"When, now?"

He sighs, makes a stretching noise. She can picture him sprawled on his bed, the dark blue bedspread in mounds and twists. "No, after work. But then I woke up and didn't feel like getting out."

"You could have let me know."

"Who's there?" Damante asks.

"Maggie, David, Carolyn, and Jess."

"Order the hummus and cheese platter."

"We had the crab sticks," she says.

"Aw, man."

Her heel is burning. "So you're not coming?" Terri hates her voice at that moment.

"I don't think so." He yawns, politely excuses himself. "Listen, have a great time. Get the red velvet cake."

"Diet," she reminds him.

"You don't need that."

She walks a few steps and glances into the restaurant. Maggie notices her and gives her the "what's happening?" signal—shoulders hunched, hands upturned.

"Maybe I'll come by after?" she says.

"What time?"

"Soon."

"I think that's a good idea," he says.

Terri walks back to the table, trying to ignore the pain in her right foot. She flags down the waiter and orders another Cosmopolitan. Her friends continue their conversation. They know where she was and who she called, but they're all too nice to make a big deal out of it. In fact, she wonders about the determined way they are avoiding the topic, the downturned eyes when she sat down and dropped her phone onto the table.

They are younger than she is. They all work at Spa Energe and in the eleven months Terri's been there, they've had many evenings like this one. They're a gang, a team. They hit happy hours or movies at the mall. They try new, trendy restaurants. They go dancing. David and Carolyn are masseuses, and Maggie and Jess are estheticians like her. Damante works part time as a masseuse and Terri has been dating him for four months. If you could call it that.

In the parking lot, her Mercedes makes a pleasant chirping noise when she presses the button. Like a large, silver-toned pet. It, too, is part of her new life. When she landed the job at Spa Energe, a very reputable place in Newport Beach, she celebrated by selling her car and leasing the sporty car with leather seats. Tyler wanted to keep the old Honda, but he was still three years away from driving. Your dad can help with that when the time comes, she told him. As if Randy would. He was living high on the hog, down at the beach most nights and already on his third girlfriend since the divorce became final. Leaving her for someone else was insult enough but now it seemed as if he'd left her for *anyone else*. However, he was reliable with child support. That, along with a second mortgage on the house, had enabled her to finish the esthetician program quickly and keep everything afloat.

She remembered walking onto the Mercedes lot, her heels clicking on the cement, and the way the salesmen had rushed her. It felt a little premature to get the car before she'd even started the job, but she wanted to make a good impression and when it came right down to it, she felt entitled. Besides, she had shown *some* restraint. She had leased what the salesman called the "entry-level model" (as though it was Terri's job now to climb the Mercedes ladder to bigger and better cars) and she'd refrained from adding several extras. Really, the payment wasn't much more than what she'd pay for a nice Honda Civic and she needed a reliable car.

As she turned into Damante's apartment complex, her phone rang. Digging around in her purse, she parked the car and found it. "Hello?"

"Mom?"

"What's wrong?"

Karly's voice was agitated. "I thought you told Tyler to watch the movie with me, but Josh came over, and they're in his room with the door locked. It's so quiet in there, and now I'm sort of freaked out because it feels like I'm here alone. They're on the computer, I think. Probably watching porn."

"Karly."

"Okay, I don't know what they're doing but why can't they open the door?"

Terri checks her makeup in the rearview mirror. "Watch the movie by yourself. I'll be home in about an hour. You should be in bed by then anyway."

"*I know*, Mom. Aren't you going to talk to him?"

"I'm at dinner, Karly. I thought you could handle being left alone. All your friends stay home alone, you said. Twelve is the legal age, you told me. Remember?"

"It's just that Tyler—"

"All right," Terri says. "Knock on his door and tell him I said Josh has to leave by nine-thirty. Then you're in bed by ten, right?"

Her voice goes up an octave. "When are you coming home?"

"Probably ten-thirty. I'll tuck you in."

"Bye."

Terri locks her car with another pair of chirps and goes to Damante's door. Everything is the same as the last time she came—the three empty pots on his neighbor's porch, the netting of spider webs under the awning—and yet, there's been a shift in the earth. She can feel it.

He opens, and she tucks herself under his arm. He rubs her back, reaches around with his other hand to shut the door.

"Did you have the red velvet cake?" he wants to know.

"No, I skipped."

"Mistake," he says.

She sits next to him on the sofa, where he's been watching a baseball game. They've talked about this, his love of baseball and Tyler's experiences with Little League. Damante played in high school. She imagines he's gained weight since then; his body is soft in places but muscular underneath. Broad shoulders but a belly that poofs slightly over his belt. Randy was always so lean, all gristle from so many days of surfing. But there was no comparison between them, not really.

"Do you want anything?" Damante asks. "Water? Something else?"

"No, thanks," she says. Leaning against him on the couch, she remembers the first time she came here, his offers of food, drink, a warm shower. It was so unlike most men she'd known, especially young men. He said his mother had a lot to say about hospitality while they were growing up. She'd been a single mother like Terri was now, with three boys and a full-time nursing job all along. Damante didn't talk about her often, or about his family, but when he did, Terri perked up. This woman, his mother, seemed to have done something right by him.

"I'm going to get some water," he says, leaving her on the couch, the side of her body cooling from his absence.

"Carolyn took that rescheduled massage today," she says. "You know what? On second thought, do you have any wine?"

"Nope," he says from the kitchen. "A beer?"

"Sure."

He comes back into the room, looks around, then sits across from her on a chair she knows from experience to be very uncomfortable. Something his roommate bought from Ikea then didn't assemble properly. He hands her the beer across the coffee table.

"Are you mad about something?" she says.

He props each elbow on a knee and leans toward her. "No, I have something to tell you."

Here it comes, she thinks, and the whole thing rushes back. That club, that first night. The beige and white dress that fit her so perfectly and the way their bodies moved together on the dance floor. Everyone was watching. She had forgotten how much attention she used to get, back when she was younger, before she got married. It wasn't that she missed it; she'd been quite happy with Randy, with the kids. She'd just forgotten, and it felt good, that night, the people watching them under the golden lights. Damante's broad shoulders and creaseless, perfect skin. His beautiful, young face and brown eyes. Her astonishment when he pulled her to the dance floor and put his hands on her hips. The way her body curved into his. And later, the dinners out and nights they stayed in. He was fun and very funny. She laughed so often, so hard, and they never ran out of things to say. They'd sit around watching television, and she'd have the best time and eventually, they'd go to the bedroom but that was never the main thing. It was perfectly nice, sometimes even hot; really, for a young man of twenty-four, Damante's love-making skills were basic and unadventurous. The companionship, the energy she felt in his company, that was something else.

"I'm moving to Idaho," he says.

She takes a long drink of beer. "Idaho?" The room buzzes around her.

"My cousin Shane hooked me up with a job. Fast money, lots of it. Hard work, digging or something, but I can make five thousand a month. Six months, maybe longer. I could do so much with the money."

"That sounds horrible," she says, unable to help herself. "You'll be out in the sun all day. Why don't you ask for more hours at the spa?"

"It's not what I want to do," he says. "You know that."

"You want to dig ditches?"

He gets up, comes back to the couch. He touches her leg. "What did you think would happen?"

She grabs his hand. "You'll be back, right?"

Damante's head drops onto his chest, then he raises it to meet her eyes. "I'm really glad I met you, Terri. It was great and all, but there never was going to be more. You didn't think there'd be more?"

"Because I'm older," she says.

"Maybe," he says. "You're not settled. You want to be out when I want to stay in. I'm a homebody, you know that."

"But you're leaving!"

"That's different." He scratches his neck. "You know I can't work that job. It's not me. I took the training because it came my way and it's been all right, but I haven't seen anything. I haven't done anything."

Terri nods and turns until she's nestled in the warm curves of his body. His arm comes around her and his hand settles on her hip. "You're right," she says. "This is your chance. An adventure." She sighs. "You've always been the mature one. You're wise beyond your years, Damante."

"I don't know about all that," he laughs.

She wants to say things like we'll keep in touch or you can call me when you get there or please don't ever forget me. And she realizes that now, she'll never meet his mother, this woman who has become a symbol, a road Terri can navigate if only she tries. She wants to say I'll be forty in a few years, but she knows him well enough, knows he will scoff and dismiss the comment and she knows also that she should aspire to his clarity. She wants to say everything and says nothing. This arm is enough, she thinks, this body, this warmth.

And when her cell phone rings and she sees that it's her children again, calling from home and expecting her there, she kisses Damante, wishes him luck, and closes the door softly when she leaves.

CHAPTER

15

Hallowicz

Girl Seeks God

In the kitchen, her father stood near the stove, his legs apart some distance and his elbows moving. The air was pungent, thick, salted. Steam swirled in wispy clouds near the ceiling and blurred at eye level.

"Betsy girl," he said, noticing her. "Get me a rag."

She detoured to the sink and handed him a damp cloth, which he used to wipe the bacon grease from the counter. Before he did this, he put a utensil on the countertop, long-handled with a round screen, and it dripped there. He picked it up, placed it over the crackling skillet of meat, and wiped again with the rag. Then he threw the cloth over his shoulder, grease and all.

"You're ruining that," she said.

His forehead was slick with sweat. "You sound like your mother," he said. "Next you'll tell me bacon stinks up the house."

She reached around and grabbed a cooked piece from a nearby plate. "No, I like it," she said. "What is that thing?"

"This?" He lifted the strange utensil slightly. "It's a splatter guard. Keeps the grease in the pan."

Her father was a sucker for gadgets and tools. He had a metal device to grill hot dogs perfectly, a contraption for coiling the garden hose so that it never kinked, and a television antennae it took him an entire Saturday to install on the roof. And on Sundays, he liked to cook breakfast.

She didn't want to mention that the grease was actually everywhere—on the rag, the stove, the counter—so she said instead, "You'll smell like bacon at church."

"God will like that," he said. With tongs, he pinched two slices and moved them toward the plate, dripping more grease onto the counter. "Everybody knows heaven smells like bacon."

Betsy entered the hall and walked past her brother's room. The door was shut. James was fourteen and mostly unbearable. He liked to sleep late and always complained about Sunday Mass, about his "spoiled and bratty" sister, about most things in his life, really.

In her parents' room, her mother sat before the dressing table, a pale green dresser topped with a trio of mirrors. She held a lipstick container aloft as though she were deciding what to do with it.

"Mama?"

"Yes?" She turned back to the mirror and twisted the lipstick open.

A bright coral color, Betsy could see, which didn't seem to make sense with the bird's egg blue suit draped over the bed. But her mother always looked immaculate; other women often complimented her style, her makeup, her hair. Betsy watched as she puckered and spread the lipstick.

Starting in the middle, up and around the curve of each side of her upper lip, then a steady swipe along the bottom. Lips rubbed together, then perfectly blotted onto a tissue.

At the corner of the dressing table sat a mirrored tray. On that, a variety of delicate containers. Frankincense and myrrh, Betsy always thought. She watched as her mother shifted a few around and brought forth the square bottle of amber liquid. The stopper was glass too, almost as wide as the bottle. Carefully, her mother upended the bottle then patted tiny circles of damp fragrance onto her wrists and behind each ear.

"Betsy," she said, turning again. "What is it?"

"Oh, nothing." She'd forgotten why she came in. "I need to get dressed."

"Is your father finished cooking?" she asked.

"Not yet."

"Crack that window for me, will you?" She turned back to the mirror and leaned in with her mascara. "He'll stink up the whole house."

Betsy turned the crank until the window separated from the wall with a sucking sound. A puff of chilled air traveled up her arm. "Still cold outside," she said.

"It's June," her mother said. "Can't last forever."

But she had her doubts. Every year, the summer seemed shorter and the winter more miserable. The plants were beginning to bloom, but many mornings, the frail petals were covered in frosty dew. Dampness pervaded the house; she still slept with two blankets. She liked the winter when it started, the snow the first few times it fell. It just went on for too long. There had to be sunnier places than Wisconsin, she often thought.

Within an hour, they were standing outside the brick church, and it had warmed considerably. Her brother leaned against the wall in a shady area as her parents chatted with another couple. He scowled at her when she looked over. She walked to a planter near the church entrance. In the center, a white-mantled Virgin Mary, her hands upturned under folds of plaster robe. Flowers had been recently added around her feet, and the earth was dark and rich. Betsy got distracted by the aroma of the blooms—sweet, like lemon or no, honey. They smelled like honey in a cup of tea, she was thinking—and she didn't notice when her parents had walked into the church. James called her name and embarrassed, she hurried to follow.

They sat in the sixth pew. They always sat in the sixth or seventh pew, on the outside instead of the center. Her father, her mother, Betsy, and James at the end. In fact, her brother stopped to let her pass, to assume her place. She kneeled and rushed through a couple of prayers, not really thinking but taking inventory of the families, the dresses, the flowers at the altar.

They sat back and her mother held her wrist for a moment, her thumb tracing circles on Betsy's skin. Everything was quiet and anticipation, order and habit. Her father leaned forward to wink at her, then he folded his hands onto his lap. Shortly, the organist announced the start of Mass with a few prolonged chords. They rose, and when she saw the swinging chain, the gold vessel spewing smoke, she burrowed into her mother's side, taking deep breaths of her fragrance, which could mask the intrusion of the incense and which, however comforting, was too unique and complex to name.

Boy Grows Up

There was a woven basket for Amanda's and a metal bell for Joshua's, and two tiny license plates with their names, smaller versions of the New Mexico one on his own car. They were common names, it turned out. Kathy was always able to find them on beaded bracelets and souvenir mugs, on tee shirts and hats. They hadn't chosen the names for such practical reasons, only because they appealed. At the time, it seemed like the pure way to do it, without obligation, without guilt, but Robert had second-guessed this decision from time to time.

The New Mexico license plate had colors intended to signify the landscape—deep orangey red, greens, and browns. He would affix the plates to a clamp that tightened around the bar under the padded seat. Or maybe they should go on the front? He'd have to ask Kathy.

The twins were turning seven; it was hard to believe. How many times had he heard from more experienced parents, trying to be helpful: Pay attention. It'll go so quickly. They'll be in high school before you know it. First grade was a long way from high school but still, it had passed in a flash.

"Sleeping on the job?" Kathy came into the garage, closing the door quietly behind her.

He looked over and noticed she had changed into a fitted pair of jeans and yellow shirt. "You look nice," he said.

"Charmer," she said, handing him a pen, then two greeting cards. "Sign."

Amanda and Joshua had already had a party the previous Saturday, the entire first grade class at a local park in a windstorm. Kathy chased freed balloons and party napkins all afternoon, while he took charge of the hot dog and hamburger production at the grill. But today was the actual day of their birth, their *real* birthday, the twins would say. And they would be surprised with new bicycles.

Kathy waited while he signed the cards, one hand resting lightly on his shoulder. He knew she wanted to say something but appreciated that she didn't. From the moment she suggested the bicycles, she'd been cautious yet casual. Waiting to see what he would do or say.

"Should I bring them around to the front?" he asked her.

She rubbed her hands together, her eyes shining. "Yes, on the walkway, don't you think? They'll see them when we leave for school." She took the cards back from him.

"Give me twenty minutes. Oh," he said, holding up the license plates. "Do these go on the front or the back?"

"The back," she said. "So people can see them." Something flashed across her face, very briefly. "I'll listen for the garage door, then we'll come out."

His face was turned away when she left. Angrily, he wiped his sleeve across his eyes.

He took the bikes outside one at a time, parked them next to each other on the curved walkway that split their rock yard into two equal halves. It was a picture of perfect symmetry. Two adults, two children.

A piercing squeal cut into the morning air, and Amanda rushed forward in a blur of purple and pink. She was a slightly plump girl with a generous smattering of freckles and the red-brown hair she got from her mother. Robert often imagined she was just as Kathy had been as a girl: rambunctious, honest, free. Behind her came Joshua, dark hair and slim build, more reserved but grinning and looking back and forth from his mother to his father for confirmation.

Robert pushed the blue bicycle with its long chrome handles toward his son. "This one's yours."

Amanda had thrown her backpack down and was already climbing onto her pink model.

"We should lower the seat a little, honey," Kathy said.

"No, it's good," she said. "I want to go!"

Both children had some experience on bicycles, but their old ones were equipped with training wheels and as far as Robert knew, they hadn't been on them for some time. Joshua held his new bike by the rubber-covered handles, looking up at his dad.

Amanda was already halfway down the driveway; her mother ran alongside, steadying her with one hand on the back of her seat.

"What do you think?" Robert asked Joshua. "Wanna give it a try?"

"Not yet," he said. "Maybe after school."

"Come on, let's try it out. I'll hold on. See how Mommy's holding Amanda?" He took the bike out of his son's hands and lifted the kickstand with his foot. "Just jump on."

"We have to go to school," Joshua said, clenching the straps of his backpack, which was still on his back.

"We have time," Robert said. "I won't let go." He reached over and tried to remove the backpack.

Joshua struggled, just a little, then let him. He climbed up and his toes barely grazed the cement. "It's too high," he said.

"No, it's fine." Robert started pushing and the bicycle swerved from side to side. "Hold it straight!" he said.

"I can't," the boy said. "It's too fast."

"You can do it," he said. "I've got you."

"I don't want to," Joshua whined. "Stop, stop!"

Robert stopped pushing as Kathy and Amanda came back up the drive. His wife's face was pink with effort and his daughter's hair was blown away from her face. Both were smiling.

"What's wrong?" Kathy asked.

"He won't let me," Robert said, his voice cracking.

And she helped Amanda down from her bicycle and pulled the girl toward her brother, who was standing to the side, trying not to cry. She grabbed Joshua by the sleeve and brought him along too, until they were all huddling around Robert on the rocky ground, holding him up.

16

Hanley/Gleeson

A Family Reunion

"There she is." Janet peered through the windshield, squinting behind her metal-framed glasses. "Oh, look at her."

Kizzy veered around the tail end of a limousine protruding into her lane. "Where? I don't see them." And as she said that, she did. Lurie in a brightly colored shawl, too heavy for the California weather, Brandon alert and searching each passing car. Lurie's brown hair was long and straight, her face full and youthful. Kizzy ran a hand over her own darker, shorter hair.

"Pull in there," Janet said, fidgeting now in her seat.

By the time Kizzy had the car in park, her mother had leapt out and was hugging Lurie. "Look at you," she heard her say. "Just look at you."

Brandon leaned into the opened passenger side door and nodded at Kizzy. "Pop the trunk?" His face was red, as though already slightly burned in the ten minutes they'd stood on the curb. His blonde hair was combed back, a conservative cut as always.

She pressed the button, and the car bounced when he hoisted the suitcase in. Slowly, Lurie lowered herself into the backseat.

"You're massive," Kizzy said.

Lurie moved across the seat in concerted, small movements. She reached up and squeezed Kizzy's shoulder. "Thanks for picking us up."

Janet got back in and turned to face Lurie. Kizzy noticed they'd both started crying. She looked away.

"It's warm," Brandon said. "Won't be needing this." He tucked a gray jacket next to him.

Away from the terminal, the cars picked up speed. Kizzy maneuvered to the left lane that would take her out to Wilshire, then back to the freeway.

Janet was rooting around in her purse. She found a tissue, shook it out, then dabbed at her eyes. "You look great, Lurie. How are you feeling?"

"Fine, Mom. Fat and slow. Just a regular pregnancy, I guess."

"You look like you're due any day," Kizzy said, glancing in the rearview mirror.

"No, she doesn't," Janet said.

"She likes giving me a hard time," Lurie said. "It's what she does."

"The doctor said her weight gain is perfectly within expectations," Brandon said. "In fact, at the ultrasound the other day, he told her she looked fantastic."

"You had an ultrasound?" Their mother twisted around again. "Do you know what it is?"

Lurie laughed. "Well, it's a *baby*, Mom."

"You know what I mean."

Kizzy tapped her fingers on the steering wheel. "It's probably a girl. All those years of makeup and hair preparation have to pay off."

Lurie poked her older sister in the shoulder. "Wouldn't have hurt *you* to do something with your hair once in a while. Mom, everything's fine, but I want to know how you're doing."

Janet turned back to face the front. "I'm glad you girls are both here."

"We want to help," Lurie said. "What can we do, I mean, for the memorial or at the house? The last thing we want is to make more work for you this week, Mom."

"Everything's under control," Kizzy said. "There'll be a short service at church, then a ceremony at the gravesite for those who want to come. A few people will follow to the house from there."

"Food? Cleaning? There must be something—"

"He'd want you to have his golf clubs, Brandon."

They all looked at Janet.

"I hope you can arrange to have them shipped, or I'm sure you can check them on your flight back. He just bought those clubs last year. They're very expensive."

"Thank you, Mom," Brandon said.

Kizzy saw a look exchanged in the backseat.

"Mom," Lurie said. "Dad is much taller than Brandon. I'm not sure—"

"No, it's great," he said.

"Was," Kizzy said. "Dad *was* much taller."

"Shit, Kizzy," Lurie said.

Janet sighed. "Well, have a look at them while you're here."

They rode in silence for a while. Once they were on the 405, Kizzy maneuvered to the carpool lane, which was moving slightly faster than the other lanes. They went under an overpass and were shrouded in shade momentarily, then the sun smacked into the car again.

Janet cleared her throat. "There's something I want to discuss with you girls, and I don't know what the right time is."

"Mom—" Kizzy started. She hoped it wasn't going to be about her father, about his disloyalties or anything else he may have done. He wasn't perfect, but she didn't want to hear about it just then. Not with Lurie and Brandon in the car. Not today.

"What is it, Mom?" Lurie asked.

"There's this woman, Penny. She lives in Ohio and several years back, she contacted your father, then me."

Heat rose in Kizzy's face. Penny? Another one?

"She's his sister," Janet said. "His half-sister."

"What?" Lurie lurched forward on the seat. "How come we never heard about her?"

"You know that Daddy's father took off when he was young. Apparently, he married another woman in Ohio and had two daughters there."

"You talked to this woman?" Kizzy asked.

Janet nodded. "Years ago. Your father didn't want anything to do with her, but I felt sorry for her. Wait, that's not true. We became friends, sort of. She was a nice lady, but your father found out I was talking to her and then I stopped."

"Shit," Lurie said again.

"What did she want?" Brandon asked. "Money?"

"No," Janet said. "No, she wanted to know Glen. Anyway, I'm telling you this for two reasons. First, do you think I should give her a call, after all these years, and tell her about your dad? Second, in case either of you had any interest in getting to know her."

"I don't," Kizzy said. "*Grandpa Albert* was a jerk, Mom. I'm happy for him, that he had this other wonderful family after abandoning Daddy and Aunt Dina and Aunt Cheryl, but why would I want to talk to her?"

"Actually, he left that family too. Penny had no idea where he was."

Brandon gave a protracted whistle. "Who knows how many wives he's had!"

"It's not funny," Lurie said.

Before she could help it, Kizzy spurted a tiny giggle. "They could make a reality show about him. Grandpa Albert marries across the U.S."

"Who does that?" Janet said, chuckling.

Laughter washed over them, crazy, sharp-sounding, painful. After some time, it died away.

"Oh, Kizzy," Lurie said. "I got a wedding invitation from Sara Lomero the other day."

"You're still in touch with her?"

"Yep. You're not?"

She shrugged. "Is she in California?"

"San Diego. She's getting married in September. To a woman."

Kizzy's eyes darted to the mirror, then back to the freeway. There was something in Lurie's voice. "That's nice," she said.

"Remember when she made you that ashtray in Girl Scouts, and you were like, ten?" She turned to Brandon. "What was she gonna do with an ashtray?"

"Her parents are still there," Kizzy said. "Do you ever see them, Mom?"

"Once in a while."

"I wonder what ever happened to the Bairds," Lurie said. "Billy and Mack. They were our neighbors too," she explained to Brandon. "Mack was always trying to feel me up."

"Lurie!" Janet turned to glare at her.

"It's true! He'd corner me in the yard or push me against the fence."

"That can't be true."

"We were kids," Lurie said. "I'm not saying he molested me or anything."

"I don't remember anything like that," Kizzy said.

"Okay, okay. Calm down, you two."

"Sara was a nice girl," Janet said. "I hope she'll be very happy."

Kizzy kept her hands at ten o'clock and two o'clock on the steering wheel. Reaching over, she turned on the radio to the easy listening station. She'd have to pay attention and switch it if anything too sad came on. In the backseat, Lurie leaned against Brandon, her growing belly poking out from the colorful shawl. Janet leaned her head against the seat and closed her eyes. Outside, the day went on and on and on, blue skies and the spotlight of the sun, shimmering sparks on the hood of the car, spreading like butter on the long stretch of freeway. And Kizzy drove on, watching and waiting for her exit.

Woman Chooses Career

A group of men huddled around a buffet table laid with pastries, fruit, coffee and tea. Near the door to the conference room, Tom Blackstone stood talking to a woman, someone Susan didn't know, but he looked over as she made her way across the patterned carpet.

"Susan Gleeson! It's about time you showed up."

Several of the men near the breakfast spread looked over. She stopped near Tom and put her hands on her hips. "Now, what do you mean by that, Tom? I'm usually one of the first to arrive and you know that."

The woman—small, with birdlike features and pointy elbows—reached for Susan's hand. "I'm Michelle Hill."

Susan thought about all the business articles she'd read, about how women should dress if they wanted to be taken seriously, about how they should grasp and shake a hand firmly. This woman, with her serious demeanor and dark blue suit, seemed to be a graduate of that school of thought. She extended her own hand with its jangly bracelet and sure enough, Michelle Hill gripped and shook it with a great deal of force and seriousness. Susan purposely kept her own hand soft and, in her opinion, ladylike.

"Susan Gleeson," she said, "as you've heard from this gentleman." She looked over at Tom, whose grin was wide and unabashed.

"Susan's leading sales this year in our office," Tom said. "She probably doesn't even need to be here. You should give all of us training, right?"

She shrugged and felt the settling of her breasts as she did. "Now Tom, I'm not sure I could teach *you* anything."

Michelle put her hands in the pockets of her skirt. "I think I'll get some tea. It was nice to meet you, Susan."

"Likewise, dear." Susan noticed her bird-like eyes narrow that. She watched as Michelle Hill walked—with no personality at all—to the table.

Tom put his hand on the small of her back. "I hear congratulations are in order," he said near her ear.

She leaned back to take him in better. He was quite tall and being next to him at this angle, peering up, she thought for a moment of Glen Hanley. "The year's not over yet, Tom."

He moved his hand a little on her back. "Not for sales. I heard you're a grandma."

Susan laid her hand on his bicep, which was surprisingly firm. "I've *been* a grandma, honey. This is number three."

"Your daughter?"

"What? No." She smiled. "My son Kristopher and his lovely wife. He's a lawyer, you know. Remember that!"

Tom cleared his throat. "I got a lawyer in my family, too, so we're even."

Susan reached up with both hands to smooth her hair and watched as Tom's eyes went to her elevated breasts. She'd been curling her hair with a flatiron the way she'd seen it done on a television commercial. Late at night, when she had trouble sleeping, after the magic cleaning solution infomercial and the costume jewelry extravaganza.

"They've had three babies in four years," she told him. "At this rate, they'll make me the grandma of ten or so."

"Oh, lord. Let's hope not."

"How much time do we have?" she asked. "I need to get some coffee in me."

"I'll get it for you," he said. "What else do you want? Something sweet?"

She looked towards the food. "A Danish? Is there lemon?"

"You go sit down," he said. "Give your feet a rest from those heels."

Susan looked down at her feet, at the beige, strappy shoes and her lean legs. She didn't see anything wrong with embracing her female side, in business or anywhere else. And wasn't she leading sales? Hadn't she sold fourteen houses already and was closing in on that apartment building? That would put her over the top for sure. Untouchable.

Tom caught her elbow in his warm hand and pulled her closer. "I'm staying at the hotel tonight," he said. "If you want to grab a drink after the presentations."

She raised her eyebrows, letting her mouth lift on one side. Keep him guessing, she told herself, although she already knew what the answer would be.

She walked over to one of the round tables set up for their informal meal. The tablecloth was long, and she had to move it aside to squeeze in. She looked up in time to see Tom Blackstone, walking over with a small plate in one hand and a white mug in the other. He grew and grew as he approached, his shoulders like a coat rack, his thick neck like a plaster column over his collar. She thought again of Glen Hanley, his large, sometimes fumbling hands and soft lips. The stale air in the hotel rooms, the lukewarm Merlot in plastic cups. She had attended his funeral, even though she hadn't seen him for some time when it happened. There was no abrupt end to their relationship, no fight or explanation, no teary farewell. Life got in the way, and it became more and more difficult to meet. Or maybe the desire had abated, but whatever the reason, their meetings spread out until one day, they quit arranging them.

At the memorial service, she sat in the final row of the church like the pariah she was, watching Janet and her keening daughters, feeling miserable. There had been a few others, but Glen Hanley held a special place. There was something so vulnerable about him, so exposed. But she'd been relieved when he quit calling; it had begun to feel like another obligation she couldn't keep.

Tom returned from the buffet and placed the pastry in front of her. "I forgot to ask. Cream or sugar?"

She looked up, his broad shoulders blocking the fluorescent lighting above until she couldn't see past him.

"Both," she said, smiling. "Always both."

CHAPTER

17

Moore

A Betrayal

Joy unlocks the front door and steps into the entryway. They'd forgotten to turn the patio light on, so she flips the switch. When she shuts the door, her eyes are blurred with tears.

She's cold. Her shirt falls just below her bra, and her stomach is exposed and covered with goose bumps. But it was warm when she put it on, earlier today. She hadn't known what to expect, hadn't known they'd be at the hospital so long, and Grandma Terri insisted on taking them to dinner afterwards. At least she kept Melinda with her. Joy said she had homework to finish and asked to be dropped off at home. Really, she just wants to be alone.

When she's halfway down the hall, she hears a jingling noise from the back. The hairs stand up on her neck. She thinks for a moment about Kitty, the cat they had for a couple of years before she ran away and never came back. Her mom had refused other pets since then; she said her heart couldn't take it.

Joy walks towards her parents' room, where a dim light is on. She steps into the doorway and a dark figure stands at her parents' dresser. A drawer is open.

"Uncle William?"

He turns and stares at her. His hair's a mess, and his eyes are bloodshot. A black hoodie is zipped up to his neck, and his jeans are torn and frazzled at the bottom.

"You look like a robber," she says.

"Hey, kid." His hands fall to his sides.

She steps into the room. "Wait. What are you doing?"

"Your mom borrowed something from me. I was looking for it." He walks toward her, but she doesn't move from the doorway.

Even from several feet away, she can smell him. Musty, like cigarette smoke and damp towels. Something swells in her. "She borrowed something from *you*? You don't even have an apartment since you got kicked out of that last one. Were you stealing from us?"

His face darkens. He pushes her shoulder and moves around her.

She follows him down the hallway. "My mom's in the hospital, Uncle William, probably *dying*, and you're here stealing from us? What, for drugs?"

He spins around. "She's not dying!" Hunched over, he walks to the front door.

Joy steps forward and pushes him. She is as tall as he is, although he's almost a decade older. He stutter-steps, recovers, then hurries outside. She turns the deadbolt and leans against the door, crying. Outside, she hears a loud sniffle, a ragged cough, then his footsteps as he runs into the night.

Woman Chooses Career

Amber makes a beeline for the bakery department, praying she isn't too late. No, there they are: a pyramid of plastic containers on a front table. Inside each one, undecorated sugar cookies in assorted shapes—ghosts, pumpkins, bats. She grabs two containers and heads toward the frosting on Aisle 9.

The mothers with more organizational skills and housekeeping talents probably baked their own. They probably found cookie cutters and had already arranged the cookies on wax paper for the kids to decorate. She has no excuse, really, now that she hasn't been working for a while. But sometimes, she goes back to bed after getting Melinda to school; today, she slept until ten o'clock. Psychologists would say she was depressed, she knew that. But she considered it more of a short hibernation period. Taking stock, deciding on a new course.

She has volunteered to help at the Halloween party for Melinda's class, which starts in twenty minutes. She also signed up to bring cookies. Her daughter must have reminded her five or six times yesterday, and again this morning. Melinda is only ten but wise to the fact that her mom's slipping a little.

There are two women in the express lane, which is manned by a cashier Amber knows to be quick. She puts her items on the conveyer and sneaks a peek at her phone.

Fifteen minutes left, and a text from Tyler. The text is an hour old. She had turned the sound off when she crawled back into bed. "Lunch?" it says.

"What time?" she answers as her cookies lurch ahead on the black rubber.

The woman in front of her is having a conversation about cantaloupe. Amber taps her foot impatiently.

"12:30?" Tyler texts.

"1:00?" she types.

The cashier is very fast, and Amber is headed outside before Tyler answers again. "Perfect," he puts. And then, "Meet at office."

Tyler's job has been a constant throughout the twelve years of their marriage. Amber has had three, all general office work, and she was recently laid off from the investment firm where she was a secretary for five years. She's been on a few interviews, but nothing has panned out yet.

She makes it to the third-grade classroom as the other parents are spreading purple and orange tablecloths onto rectangular tables. She doesn't remember the color purple having such a dominant role in Halloween when she was growing up. Melinda's face lights up, and she waves when she sees her mother. Because Amber has already raised one daughter, she knows to appreciate this. Soon enough, Melinda will be too conscious of what her friends think; soon enough, she'll want as much time away from Amber as she can manage.

She and Tyler are so proud of Joy, though. She's living in Anaheim, working at a car dealership but taking classes at the community college at night. She's always been a fiercely independent girl, and there've been periods when they worried she was headed in the wrong direction. Late nights, sketchy friends. They've had horrible fights. Joy once told Amber that irresponsible behavior must be hereditary, considering how her own life started. And what could they say? But she's doing well now, even comes home almost every weekend to visit.

Amber helps pass around cans and tubes of frosting, shakes containers of edible sprinkles, and when it's all done, wipes. They send the kids to their recess all sugared up. The whole production lasts about twenty minutes, but it takes the parents longer to clean up the debris. Frosting dots the carpet near one of the tables; it's smeared on the wall by the door.

It's ten minutes until one o'clock when Amber gets back into her car. She has eaten nothing all morning except for a quick cup of instant coffee and half of a frosted sugar cookie someone left behind. Her stomach is queasy. She thinks about being pregnant with Melinda. She spent three months in a perpetual state of nausea, but it didn't stop her from eating everything in sight. She'd have breakfast with Tyler and Joy, then she'd drive through some place and have a second breakfast after she dropped Joy at school. She gained sixty pounds, and it hadn't been easy to lose the weight after Melinda was born. But they'd been happy, and worried, having tried to get pregnant for so long. The tests, the treatments, the endless progesterone shots Tyler administered in their tiny master bathroom. She was stress-eating through the pregnancy, she realized that now. Just as she's stress-sleeping now.

Tyler is standing outside the brick building, so she pulls up next to the curb to pick him up. He leans over and kisses her cheek. "You smell like frosting. Did you remember to take the cookies?"

"Yes," she says. "I had enough reminders, didn't I?"

His eyes widen. "Sorry. Did Melinda have fun?"

"She wanted to save her cookie for after lunch. She's such a funny kid. You should have seen all the others shoving them in as fast as they could."

"Turn here," Tyler says.

Amber takes a right at the next intersection. "Where do you want to eat? I'm starving."

"Someplace new," he says.

And he directs her towards the east side of town, farther than they've ever gone for a simple lunch. There are countless restaurants within two miles of the business sector where he works. Tyler is peering through the windshield, watching the small businesses pass by.

She has a bracing thought, that his patience may, in fact, have its limits. After everything he did throughout her cancer, his endless support during their fertility treatments and the breakdown she'd almost had when she realized enough was enough. Now, she needed to pull herself together again.

"Okay, wait," he says. "Here, turn in here."

They've arrived at a small strip mall, anchored by a Vons at one corner and a Starbucks at the other. "What's here?" she asks.

"Park anywhere," he says.

When she gets out of the car, he takes her hand and pulls her along, past a dry cleaner and a noodle restaurant, until they're standing in front of a small flower shop. Early Blooms, it's called. He stops and turns her toward him.

"This place is for sale. An elderly couple have had it for eighteen years, and they're retiring. Everything you'd need is there, and they would help the new owner with suppliers, procedures, stuff like that. And there's a customer list, existing customers. You'd just basically step in and start running it."

"*I* would?" she says. "What do you mean?"

"You've always talked about this," he says. "I called Bank of America. We could get a start-up loan. I spoke to Gerry at work, you know his wife has her own decorating business. Anyway, he's been helping me figure everything out—taxes, business license. It's doable, that's all I'm saying." He puts his hands on her shoulders. "If you want," he says.

Amber looks again at the store. Metal shelves hold buckets of flowers behind the window. She can imagine the sound of the bell the owners have tied to the handle of the door. She can imagine getting her morning coffee at Starbucks and settling into the cozy store. There will be so much to learn. She knows nothing about flower arranging, nothing about having a business.

"Are you sure we can afford it?" she asks. "Is this the right time?"

His face widens into a grin—smug as a jack-o-lantern. "When have we ever worried about that?"

A Love Story

Terri smooths the white napkin over her lap. "This is nice, Maggie. Thank you."

"What's that saying, old friends are the best, something like that?"

"And by 'old,' you mean friends for a long time?"

She laughs. "Of course! Sorry, did I call you old on your birthday?" She lifts her glass of white wine. "Cheers, girlfriend."

Terri clinks her glass against Maggie's. Actually, she has a little headache from her overindulgences the night before, but she doesn't want to ruin the special lunch her friend has planned.

Maggie adjusts her pink cardigan and reaches for the bread. She's in her late fifties, but her face is barely lined, just around the mouth and a few crow's feet. One of the benefits of working in skin care for so long, Terri thinks. "That color is great on you," she says.

"Why, thank you. Your birthday was Saturday?"

"Yesterday," Terri says.

"What did you do?" She takes a bite of the bread, smeared thickly with butter.

Terri feels her face get warm. "The kids took me out for dinner. Karly and Mike, Tyler and Amber. The grandkids. Joy couldn't make it. She's studying for her final exams. She'll graduate in a few weeks."

"You look flushed," Maggie says.

She takes a sip of her wine. "Randy came, too," she says.

Maggie's eyes widen. "And?"

"We had a nice dinner. Italian. Rosa's Bistro, have you been there? I took a break from my diet and had the rigatoni. They have a sautéed mushroom appetizer. I've never seen mushrooms cooked quite like this. They were slightly breaded and served with a cheese dip—"

"You know what I mean."

Terri lifts her shoulders. "What?"

"You told me he was flirting with you the last time you saw him. What was it, a pool party?"

"Melinda's birthday. You know, she's the best violinist in her school. She's going to travel to the Midwest somewhere for a competition." Terri leans back in her chair, holding her wine glass.

"Would you like to order, ladies?" The waitress is young and bright-faced.

Maggie rolls her eyes at Terri then orders a chicken and provolone panini.

"Cobb salad for me," Terri says.

"Is this a special occasion?" the waitress asks.

"As a matter of fact," Maggie says, raising one eyebrow. "It's my friend's *sixty-seventh* birthday."

Terri narrows her eyes.

"Wow," the waitress says. "You look great."

"Thank you."

"Bitch," Terri says after she leaves. Then she waits for the perfect moment, right when Maggie has lifted the water glass to her mouth, right when she takes a long drink—

"Randy came home with me after dinner," she says.

Maggie sputters her water. "I knew it!"

She leans forward. "It was so strange, Maggie. And not strange. Does that make sense?"

"Perfect sense."

"We had too much wine at dinner, probably. I'm sure he's kicking himself this morning."

"He's not."

"He volunteered to drive me home because he had come with Tyler and Amber. Of course, we have to keep it from the kids." She shakes her head. "At this point, I don't even know what 'it' is."

Maggie puts her hand on Terri's arm. "My friend, *it* is what it always was. And your kids are in their forties! They probably already know."

Terri sips her wine and thinks, sips and thinks. To be so old and yet so new, she thinks. No time to waste and all the patience in the world. And her thoughts turn to her cobb salad because as it turns out, she's pretty hungry after all.

CHAPTER

18

Hallowicz

Family Survives Tragedy

In the end, it all came down to impressions, to the imperfectly remembered feelings, and details, and the feelings about the details. He had a knapsack, one he'd picked up at the Army surplus store on Artesia Boulevard. Doughboys Surplus, it was called, and the store had been there as long as Robert could remember. On the way over, his father told him he'd bought his first pair of Levis there for three dollars. He was fifteen years old, he said, and had just spent the summer milking cows and shoveling shit at one of the dairy farms on his father's delivery route.

Robert and Wilson drove in the roofing company truck, a newer Ford loaded down with supplies that creaked and rattled as they went. The day was sunny, but weren't they all? When Robert thought back on his ending childhood, few memories were framed with anything other than blue skies and blooming plants all around. There was a party once, for his brother, with typhoon-like rains that forced a gaggle of children into his mother's unfussed kitchen. But those damp days were rare.

They drove under the sun, then, as his father remembered the stench of the cows, his own father's melodic humming, the stiff Levis that softened and wrinkled with every wash. Shrink to fit, he said, and they meant it. He told Robert about the Mexican-American War, the dust-covered soldiers returning from the dry terrain of northern Mexico and how they'd resembled uncooked loaves of floured bread. Doughboys. Can you imagine, his father said, shaking his head. The heat, he said.

The store itself was dark and crowded with supplies. Canvas jackets hung from hooks near the ceiling; wooden shelves were crammed with pants fashioned from the same rough material, clothing in the green puzzle-work pattern of camouflage, and of course, Levis.

They walked by two young men, both clean-shaven and crew-cut like Robert. He squared his shoulders, and they looked up from a display of pocketknives as he passed. He remembered that moment, their eyes meeting, the brief comprehension and unspoken complicity. Two rough-looking men, with reddened skin and biceps straining their tight t-shirts. The type of guys Robert may have avoided at one point; in the past, he may have averted his gaze.

In the back of the store, they chose a duffel in the standard faded green. The bag stood about three feet tall, with a handle on one side and backpack straps on another. A zipper went around the whole thing in case you wanted to open it all the way. His father paid with cash, always with cash, a habit Robert carried into his adult life.

Those were the impressions: sunshine, the clattering truck bed, the dairy farm, doughboys, two Army recruits, his father's crisp twenty-dollar bill. Robert loved the duffel bag as he'd never loved another inanimate object. Once he'd made it to South Carolina for basic training, the duffel stayed under his cot and sometimes during the night, he'd reach down and hold onto one of the straps. It helped him sleep. But for then, for that first ride home, the duffel bounced around in the back of the truck with the roofing supplies, picking up its first grease marks and scratches.

At the house, the mood was funereal. In fact, everywhere that day was the memory of Stevie, of the dark house in the days following the accident, of the residue that remained like soot after a flood. His mother hadn't opened the curtains in the front room. This, she usually did in the morning before Robert woke up. At least, he assumed she did because he rarely saw his father deal with anything in the house. Changing an occasional hard-to-reach bulb, reigniting the furnace pilot light, lifting and carving the Thanksgiving turkey—these irregular tasks were his domain whereas his mother dealt with the daily, the ritual, the constant. When he tried to think back on that time, the haze of childhood and its memories, his mother was a blurred but reliable presence. In the background, moving from room to room, folding clothes and arranging things in drawers. She was the soothing whirr of the vacuum and the steaming pots of beef and pasta and soup. She was the reason the tea kettle never whistled a moment too long.

That day was different, though. There was a stillness that made him think of the occasional times she'd been sick. She was down with pneumonia once—he was eleven—and he and his father had been forced to burn eggs and clean their clothes for school and work. He remembered the relief he felt that first day he found the curtains open and her resolute frame at the sink, re-washing the silverware.

He went to his room. The suitcase she had brought down from the attic was still on the bed. Seeing it gave him a pang of guilt, as though it was his fault he couldn't go to basic training with a suitcase. It wasn't a trip to Niagara Falls, was it? And he had tried to tell her nicely, but still her face pinched up. There wasn't much to pack—a few books, a small bag of toiletries, a thin photo album, assorted civilian clothes. When he came back, he'd be a soldier and not just their son anymore.

The photo album was from his father, given with the understanding it was from him alone. Quickly, Robert flipped through it, careful not to linger on any one image, then he slipped the album between two pairs of jeans in the duffel. The day was heavy and still then, he remembered that. Silence like oppression. His ears strained for something, anything, and it wasn't unlike many other afternoons, many other sunny times, so many days in that house.

It had been June, the start of a ruined summer. Back when warm days began with the smell of grass and sugary breakfast cereal wolfed down in front of the television. Between cartoons, glimpses from the morning's news of Vietnam. Robbie barely watched, having no interest in this war that had been going on as long as he could remember. For all the evening news updates and "interruptions from regularly scheduled programming," he had no idea what it was for or why people were so worked up by it. He only knew that any mention of the war diverted from whatever he was watching at that moment. After all, he was only six years old. Stevie was four.

They'd both had birthdays in May, Robbie's on the twelfth and Stevie's a week later on the twentieth. Two new bicycles were parked on the dirt path between the house and the fence. Their mother always said to push them further down, around the house into the backyard, or someone would steal them. Usually, they forgot. Robbie's bicycle was blue with white plastic handlebar covers and whitewall tires. Stevie's was yellow and black, with training wheels still attached; nonetheless, he could almost match his older brother in speed. *His heart goes before his head*, their father would say, and it was true: Stevie was reckless and liked to go fast and sometimes, Robbie thought the best thing would be to take his training wheels off, so he'd have to slow down for a while.

There was a gravel path in front of their house, where they were supposed to stay unless their mother came out to watch. Sometimes, she'd bring a chair and wait on the porch as they travelled up and down the street, making wide turns at the Farrells's house then zooming past. "Look!" they'd say. "Watch."

"Now get back on the path," she'd say. "I have to check on the roast." Or the meatloaf, or a casserole. Or make a phone call to Grandma Springer, or get the clothes out of the dryer. And they'd stay on the gravel, even though it kicked dirt into their eyes and left their ankles brown. Soon enough, they started testing her. One quick pass from their driveway, out to the street, up the Rivera's driveway next door, then back to the path. Every so often, Mrs. Rivera would sit on her own porch, back in the shade where they couldn't see her until they were on her driveway. She scared Robert, with her sunken cheeks and the thick black hair coiled around her head.

Robert remembered that blue and white bike and if he could isolate those days from the slew that followed, if he could recall how he felt about the bike before that certain June day, he might have said that he loved the bicycle almost as much as he'd come to love the duffel bag later. But it was hard to separate the good from the bad, the clear memories from what his adult mind and years of sadness had made of them.

The ambulance. The gnarled yellow frame. One black tire stuck upright in a bush across the street. His mother's sickening wail. The choking fear.

His father picked up pizza for dinner. Pepperoni for Robert, mushrooms and peppers for his mother, although she hardly ate. There was a wilted salad in an aluminum container, and his mother opened a bottle of red wine. The first time she'd ever served him alcohol because after all, he was still only eighteen.

She asked whether he'd be able to come home after the training. His father said he'd never been to the east coast, although he had a distant cousin in North Carolina.

This is South, Robert told him.

Outside, the streetlights were on, he remembered that. If you were outside when it happened, you could hear a pinging sound from each one. Sometimes they all came on at the same moment; sometimes, in small groups. Occasionally, one would take longer than the rest, as though it hadn't received the signal.

The bus was leaving at nine. They took turns looking at the clock while they ate their pizza. Their mother said something about the disappointment of the salad. For once, Robert took notice of her, really studied. She wore a pale green sweater and brown pants. The sweater had sleeves that ended just past her elbows, but she had pushed them up. From time to time, she blew a piece of her hair from her forehead. Her hair was brown then, before it went white, and it was wavy with short pieces in the front. A perfect gust of breath was directed from the corner of her mouth, up to the errant clump, and Robert thought how good she was at it, at that one thing. She was flushed from the wine and her eyes were shining. She must have been very pretty, he remembered thinking. His father had told him so, one time. He told Robert she was very funny and every now and then, they'd see a glimpse of her humor.

She asked about the bus trip, whether he had enough clothes, if someone would meet him when he got to the airport. He reminded her that he had the ticket already, that he'd be on his own. The night went on. He remembered when he had decided to join the Army, the assuredness he felt then and the way it had dissipated over time. But he hadn't known what else to do. And when the terrible war finally ended and he told his parents his intentions remained, his mother had cried. At thirteen, he had announced his plans and over the years, maybe she held out hope he'd change his mind. Then the war was over and perhaps she thought, ah, *that* was it, that terrible war. But he'd had the objective for so long, it felt irreversible. Chances were now, he'd never see any kind of battle, any fighting at all, but still, he wanted to go. Because he knew it would hurt her. He realized that now.

But that last night, these were the only impressions: darkness, spicy pepperoni and melted cheese, finger-smudged wine glasses, the streetlights, his mother's perfect gesture, the weighted duffel bag, his father's choked goodbye at the bus station. Because she had stayed behind to get started on the dishes, turning her back after a brief embrace. And they'd used paper plates, he remembered that, and plastic utensils from the restaurant. When the bus pulled from the station, leaving a trail of smoky puffs, he imagined her standing over the kitchen sink in her green sweater, peering through the window and into the dark, nothing to do.

CHAPTER

19

Hanley

You Can't Go Home Again

They stretched their legs and stood on the fallow ground. The house itself was in a state of renovation, with an abandoned scaffold framing the porch and plastic wrap taped over the newly installed windows.

"They're fixing it up," Glen Hanley said. He walked over and stood next to Janet and his sister, Dina, who'd come along for the ride.

"Remember the time Cheryl got stuck on the roof?" Dina asked. A tall, stocky woman, she wore a loose-fitting button-up shirt and baggy jeans. Her wrap-around black Ray Bans seemed more suited for a man.

Glen Hanley had never understood his sister's habits, why she wouldn't make any effort with her appearance. Cheryl surrounded herself with canines instead of children, but at least she wore a dress once in a while.

"What's that?" Kizzy asked.

They turned around to follow the direction of her gaze.

"The hill?" Dina said. "That's Bernal Heights Summit."

"I meant the metal thing."

"It's a radio tower." She straightened up. "We called it Nanny Goat Hill. It used to be pastureland around here, long ago, and I think the name just stuck."

Lurie stepped forward, shielding the sun from her face with her arm. "Did you ever go up there?"

"Lots of times," Dina said. "Your father used to run up and down for exercise."

"No," Glen Hanley said. His sisters always exaggerated anything he did, and it annoyed him. "I just ran around the neighborhood. We had to put in a certain amount of miles."

"Kizzy," she said. "Will you try for the cross-country team next year?" Dina was a science teacher and had been firing questions at her niece about high school all morning, since they picked her up at the little house she bought her first year out of college. She still lived there alone, still taught at the same school that hired her almost twenty years ago.

"No, probably softball."

Dina nodded. "I played volleyball, did you girls know that?" She turned to Lurie. "What about you?"

"I don't know."

"She's got a couple of years to think about it," Janet said. She walked over and stood behind Lurie who, at twelve, was just a few inches shy of her mother's height.

Glen Hanley looked at his wife and his youngest daughter and saw two versions of the same person. Why was it always so easy to see the resemblance between them, but more difficult to see any between himself and Kizzy? People always said their eldest looked just like him, but she was a girl, after all. If there was anything Glen Hanley would have liked to pass on, it would have been his athletic ability, and he'd done all right on that account where Kizzy was concerned.

They walked around the old house, peering into windows. The girls ran up to the gate.

"Can we go in the back?" Kizzy asked, already reaching for the latch.

"That's trespassing," Glen said, looking at his wife.

Janet shrugged.

"The house is empty," Dina said, charging ahead.

One thing led to another. An unlatched gate, an unlocked sliding glass door. Before long they were standing in the living room. A four-by-four was propped against one wall, but the room was otherwise empty. Just dirty walls and rust-colored shag.

"That can't be the same carpet, can it?" Dina asked.

Glen Hanley shook his head, a reflexive gesture because it felt like, at that moment, his sister was having his same thoughts. Janet had ventured down the hallway, and he followed her.

She stood in the back bedroom, which used to be his in another life. There were built-in shelves over the bed and a window that always stuck. He put his hand on Janet's shoulder, but she moved away.

"Does it make you sad to be here?" she asked.

"Not really," he said. "Are you enjoying the trip at all?" His effort to spend time with the family, to reconnect with her. This trip to make up for the nights at the bar, the flirtation with loan officer Jody that Janet didn't believe was innocent. Glen Hanley thanked God she didn't know the whole story. He thanked God that Jody had moved back to her sister's in Northridge.

Janet came away from the window and stood before him. Something had softened in her face. She touched his arm. "It seems strange that I only met your mother a few times," she said. "And you spent so much of your life here, with her."

"Time to go!" Dina's voice boomed down the hall. "You promised me lunch at the wharf!"

Glen Hanley leaned down, kissed his wife on the forehead, and led her out of his childhood room.

Boy Meets Girl

The event was being held at a local park. On the corner, there was a plastic blowup, a cartoonish yellow and white dog with a red collar.

"You're sure about this?" her mother asked.

"I love dogs," Kizzy said. "You know that."

"You loved Bruno."

She followed the line of cars into the parking lot; an attendant in an orange vest directed them to a space. "Why didn't we ever get another puppy?"

Janet's purse sat on her lap, both hands encircling the handle. "Who was going to take care of another dog? You girls were already on your way out by then."

"You and Daddy," Kizzy said.

"Yes, well."

They stepped outside and Kizzy was glad for the morning cloud cover. It would be warm enough later. Janet grabbed her elbow as they walked over the uneven dirt, which annoyed Kizzy because her mother was only in her early sixties. She kept trim, but Kizzy felt her strength was waning from lack of exercise. When they reached the sidewalk next to an expanse of grass, Janet let go.

To their left, a vendor of pet playthings had set up a table. Rubber chew toys, balls, stuffed animals like what you'd give a baby—everything laid out. On the right, a station where you could have a dog tag personalized and if you wished, studded with fake diamonds.

"Isn't that cute?" Janet said when they passed a dachshund in a pink cheetah print jumper.

Kizzy tilted an eyebrow but didn't answer.

The first pen had four dogs, all mixed-breed. One tiny black dog cowered in the corner, pawing at a frayed blanket.

"Well, hello there," a woman said. She had blonde curly hair held partially back with a blue headband, and she wore a canvas vest with "The Rescuers" in green letters.

"Good morning," Janet said. "Is it okay to pet the dogs?"

"Come here," the woman said. She put her hand out and a light brown Chihuahua sniffed it. "Like this," she told them. "You want to let them come to you first. You never want to make a sudden motion or just reach in."

Her mother exhaled loudly. "Yes, I've owned a dog before. I just didn't know if it was allowed. *That's* what I was asking."

Kizzy watched as Janet reached in and extended her hand. The dog wouldn't come.

"What's wrong with that one in the corner?" Janet asked.

The woman looked over. "Oh, she's nervous with all these people around. Normally, she's very friendly. Do you want me to try and get her to come to you?"

"No, thank you."

Janet was ten feet away before Kizzy knew to follow her and catch up. "Mom, wait. Geez."

"You don't know what it's like, Kizzy. You get old and people start to talk to you like, well, like you're senile."

"She seems like the type who talks to everyone like that."

"Well, I'm sorry. She was irritating, but we're not here for me. Let's find you a dog."

Maybe it wasn't such a good idea, Kizzy thought, maybe her mom didn't have any warm and fuzzy feelings left. Because her actual, secret plan was to try and get Janet to pick a dog.

They kept going, stopping now and then to watch the dogs in their temporary pens. It was a little sad, wondering which ones would get homes and which ones wouldn't, and Kizzy was beginning to second-guess her aims. Janet wanted to sit down, so they found a shaded bench, and she pulled a bottle of water from her purse, which she offered first to Kizzy.

"No, thanks."

"I spoke to Lurie again last night," Janet said. "She thought she may have had a contraction. She was feeling badly about her friend Amber. They were hoping to have their babies around the same time."

"Yes, that's too bad," Kizzy said. "Is she going to try again?"

Her mother nodded. "I'll have to call Lurie when we get back."

"This one should fall right out," Kizzy said.

"I hope not. Her labor with Glendon was only three hours, and she almost had Jadon on the ride to the hospital."

"At least it's a girl this time," she said.

"What does that matter?"

"It doesn't. That's just what people say, isn't it? You finally got your girl!"

Janet laughed. "They never said that to me."

At the back corner of the park, under a tree drooping with white blooms, three dogs were leashed to a pole in the ground. Two women sat on chairs nearby, petting the dogs and talking to visitors. A simple paper sign, like a For Sale sign with metal posts, was handwritten: Canine Co-op.

When Janet and Kizzy approached, a fluffy white dog bounded towards them until it reached the end of its leash and was yanked back.

"Sunflower," one of the women said. "Be careful." She stood up, and Kizzy could see that she was around her age, not quite middle-aged, with a slim build and freckled shoulders.

Janet was patting the dog, who stood now on its hind legs. She leaned over, and the dog licked her hand again and again.

"Wow," the woman said. "She really likes you."

"Her name is Sunflower?" Janet asked.

"Yes, because she's always happy." She met Kizzy's eyes then looked down. Her long blonde hair was past her shoulders.

Kizzy looked over as her mother strained to pet the dog. "Mom, why don't you sit in that chair so you can pet her." She looked at the woman. "Is that all right?"

"Of course!" She started to step out of the way at the same moment Kizzy reached for her mother's purse, and her hand touched the woman's soft middle.

"Oh, I'm sorry," Kizzy said. She leaned past her, and their arms collided again. They both laughed. Sunflower had jumped into Janet's lap and curled up into a little white ball. "Oh, Mom," she said. "I don't know how you're going to leave without her."

She blinked. "What, me?"

"I'm Sandy, by the way," the blonde woman said. "I work part-time at Canine Co-op and if you do decide to get a dog, I work as a groomer too, so I can give you a referral."

"Nice to meet you," Kizzy said. She looked at her mother, who was watching her with narrowed eyes. It made her even more nervous.

"I thought I recognized you," Janet said. "You're Sandy Gleeson."

The woman nodded. "Sandy Beltran, but yes." She looked back and forth between them. "I was married."

"Oh," Kizzy said.

"But it didn't work out."

Janet continued to watch them with a strange look, but then seemed to shake herself out of it. She lifted Sunflower to her chest and kissed her head. "Do you remember Sandy?" she asked Kizzy. "She was two grades above you, I think. Her mother and I served on the PTA together."

"Maybe," she said.

"It's okay," Sandy said. Her teeth were the whitest Kizzy had ever seen. "I'm a completely different person now."

A Legacy

"Hello?"

"What are you doing?"

"Um, sleeping."

Lurie snorted. "At ten o'clock?"

"I had a late night." Kizzy found her pajama pants at the foot of the bed.

"You?"

"Did you just call to ask annoying questions?"

"No, I called because Edon Kizzy kept me awake most of the night." She yawned as if to prove it.

"I still can't believe you named her that."

"What, Edon?"

"No, stupid."

"I didn't name her stupid."

Kizzy groaned, quietly. Next to her, there was a stirring and from the foot of the bed, Jasper had lifted his head and was waiting to see if he was going to be fed. "I have to go," she whispered.

"Wait. Is someone there?"

"Lurie."

"Oh. My. God. Someone's there." A small, braying noise came over the phone. The baby, only nine days old. "Oh, no, *it's* awake," Lurie said. "Who's there?"

Kizzy looked over. Her blonde hair was sprayed out; some of it in loops over the side of the bed. The freckles on her shoulders were reddish in the morning light. "I love you, Lurie," Kizzy said.

A short silence, then Edon cried in earnest. "I love you too, Kizzy." Lurie made shushing noises and Kizzy could picture her, bouncing the baby on her shoulder. She said her goodbyes, pulled on her pants, and slowly followed her new dog to the kitchen.

CHAPTER

20

Moore

Boy Grows Up

Melinda is already in the kitchen when I wake up. For a Saturday, this is not normal. She's even dressed, and by the looks of the crumbs around the toaster, she's had her toast already. We sometimes wonder if a girl can live on bread alone; our younger daughter seems to be living proof.

"Good morning," I tell her, and lean over to kiss the top of her head.

"Hi, Daddy," she says. One leg is bent with her foot underneath her bottom, and the other foot is on the chair. Her chin rests on her knee. It's like a very complicated yoga position.

I notice the fresh coffee, which is strange because Amber switched to tea years ago. "You're not drinking this, are you?" I ask.

She shrugs. "I made it for you."

"That was nice," I say. And I wait because surely, *something's* coming.

Melinda reaches around her knee and brings her own mug to her mouth. Hot cocoa. I can smell it now. "What are you doing today?" she asks.

"Your grandpa's coming over to help me seal those cracks in the backyard."

"What cracks?"

"In the cement."

"But they've always been there."

"That doesn't mean we have to live with them, does it?" I sit down at the table with my coffee and notice the newspaper's been brought in from the driveway.

She slides both feet onto the ground. "I can make you some eggs, if you want."

"Thanks, I'm not hungry yet." I might as well cut to the chase, or I'll never get to read the paper. "What are *you* doing today?"

She perks up at that. "Well, I wanted to talk to you. Remember how I told you Brianne's older sister has been driving for two years already? She's almost eighteen. They invited me to the beach, I think they're going to Manhattan Beach, I can find out for sure which one, and she has to take Brianne with her, their parents said, and she's allowed to invite one person and she invited me and I think we'll leave around eleven and be back by five or six, it won't even be dark or anything like that and I have everything ready so you don't have to do anything at all." She takes a breath.

I set down my cup. "What did your mom say?"

Her eyes bug out. "She said to ask you! I swear! She left early because of that wedding and I told her everything and she said to ask you because she won't be home until tonight."

"Hmm," I say.

"You can call her!"

"Okay."

"Okay you'll call Mom, or okay I can go?"

"You can go."

She jumps up and gives me an excited hug. Her hair gets in my eye for a minute because she's hopping and hugging at the same time. She smells like flowers.

"Take sunscreen," I say. "Every hour if you're in the water."

"You sound like Grandma Terri."

"And remember, you are fifteen. Not twenty-one, not eighteen."

She rolls her eyes, but only halfway. "I know."

"Wear your seatbelt and be safe."

"Thank you, Daddy, thank you!"

I watch her bound down the hall, happy that I've made her happy, even though it means I'll be worried about her all day. "And answer your phone when I call!" I yell.

"I will!"

I make myself two eggs, realizing too late I should have accepted her offer to cook them before I gave my assent. When I see what time it is, I eat quickly and take the toast with me down the hallway. I dig through the closet for an old pair of jeans and some shirt I don't mind getting dirty. I find a t-shirt with Maui on it in faded letters.

And by the time he arrives, I've already moved the patio furniture onto the grass and have swept both the rectangular slab and the walkway down the side of the house. And that's where I am when my dad lets himself in the gate. He has a bucket in one hand, a plastic bag from Home Depot in the other.

"Morning!" he says. He seems very chipper, very awake.

"Hey there," I say. When I reach for the bucket, he waves me off. I notice the slight limp as he walks toward the back. I'd ask about his leg, but he doesn't like to talk about it. I appreciate this about him, actually. Amber's parents have entered that phase of life where all they talk about are doctor appointments and medications.

He puts the supplies down in the corner of the cement slab, in the shade. Two wooden handles protrude from the bucket, and I can see there are other, shorter tools inside. From the bag, he pulls out several containers of caulk and two metal caulking guns. "This is the stuff they recommended," he says. "The guy asked me, do you need a more flexible sealer or is the area stable?" He is crouching down near the bag and looks up at me.

I notice that he's kept his bad leg extended. "What does that mean, stable?" I ask.

"Areas that are under a lot of strain, or places that shift, he said." Grunting, he stands up. "And I said, we're in California, aren't we? We're in a constant state of shifting, man!"

"Huh," I say. "Do you want some coffee?"

"Sure."

He follows me into the kitchen. "Where is everyone?"

"Melinda!" I call. But then I listen. "Sounds like she's in the shower," I tell him. "Amber went in early. She's got a wedding today."

He takes his coffee and goes to where we keep the sugar. It makes me feel good, this small thing, that he knows where the sugar is.

"She does a great job with the flower shop, that wife of yours," he says.

"Yep," I say. "I offered to help with delivery, but that new guy she hired is great. I almost feel unneeded these days. Melinda will be driving soon."

"Welcome to the world of having teenagers." He shakes his head. "What am I saying? You've already been through this once before. When will Joy be down for a visit?"

"In a couple of weeks," I say. "She's bringing someone."

"A dude?"

I smile, because it's funny to hear him say that, at his age. "Yeah, a dude."

He smiles too.

"Need something to eat?" I ask.

"No, I went down to the café this morning."

"Egg wrap?"

"Of course."

He almost always orders the egg wrap, a café original meant for the surfers, to be taken on the go. Eggs, cheese and ham wrapped in a pita-like bread. I didn't ask him if he surfed because I know he can't anymore, not really.

When we get outside, he directs the entire operation. I'm happy to let him. First, we take chisels and rubber mallets, and work our way down the line of each crack. They must be widened before they're repaired, I guess. So we get down on the ground and the clinking sound of our labors fills the air. I work for a while on my knees then sit down like he has done. The trick is to get the cracks not only widened, but angled like a V. This will allow the sealant to seep down, funnel in like a root. This is what the guy at Home Depot told him.

We work for a while without talking. He gets up once and hands me a brush with metal bristles. I know without asking it's for wiping the tiny chunks of cement out of the way, and I immediately add that to my routine. In a corner near the house, there are three initials from a previous owner carved into the cement: RJD. I'm thinking about chiseling and covering that too, but it seems like a real asshole thing to do. What if he came back one day?

"Are you still going to Hawaii this summer?" my dad asks.

I stop for a minute and wipe my forehead. The sunlight has crept to the middle of the lawn. We probably have an hour or so until we'll have to think about getting hats and sunscreen. "We're debating," I say. "Melinda wants Hawaii. I'm voting for Yosemite. I've never been there."

"And Amber?"

"Undecided. We're not sure if Joy will be able to come either, with her work schedule."

"I'd pick Hawaii," he says.

"But you've been there so many times."

"I love it." He completes one narrow crack that runs diagonally, cutting a perfect triangle into the corner of the slab. Getting up, he stretches his back. "You didn't enjoy that trip, did you?"

I look up and his head is tilted, waiting. "No," I say. "I did. I'd just like to see Yosemite."

"We had our honeymoon in Maui, your mother and me."

"I know."

"I've been seeing her, you should know that."

I stop brushing bits of concrete into a tidy pile. "What do you mean?"

He laughs. "I guess you could say we've been dating."

My parents are sixty-nine and sixty-seven, respectively. For some reason, I don't find this funny. "I don't know what to say," I say.

"Let it sink in," he says. "I've got to use your bathroom."

He almost runs into Melinda at the sliding glass door. She has curled her hair and pulled the sides back from her face. Over her bikini, she wears a fringed tank top and an equally natty pair of denim shorts. And she's in full makeup. For the beach.

My dad whistles at her, and she thinks this is very funny. Everyone thinks he's funny. Suddenly, it begins to make a little sense. Months ago, the dinner for his mother's birthday, when Amber said his father sort of invited himself along. And he gave her a ride home from the restaurant, I remember, and when I asked her about it the next day, she acted strangely.

He comes out with two bottles of water from the fridge. The sun is about five feet from the edge of the concrete. "Let's tackle the side," he says.

More chiseling, more brushing. There are less cracks, here where the cement is nestled between fence and house. Less strain than what the large, exposed piece suffers. We don't talk much, just work with our heads down. I'm whacking away on a pretty wide crack near the door that leads into the garage when all of a sudden, an army of crickets comes charging out. The chisel flies out of my hand, and I spring backwards on my hands and feet, like an upside-down spider.

My dad covers his mouth, tries not to laugh. He comes over and begins wiping the crickets out of the way with his bare hands. Just scoops them up and tries to throw them over the fence, but they're hopping and scattering all over the concrete and soon, he gives up. He looks at the crack. "I wonder how many are still down there," he says.

We get two brooms from the garage and sweep the whole area again. It's getting warmer now, and we both finish our water. We decide to do half of the caulking and then break for lunch. We cut the nozzles on the containers with a knife and put them into the guns. Leaning over, we start to fill the fissures. The stuff is chalky and gray and almost matches the color of the original cement. We fill them to the top and a little over, then we use trowels to smooth everything down. Standing up, we look over our handiwork.

"Lunch?" he asks.

I nod. We've decided to do the side section afterwards, and I'm telling myself that all the crickets will have made it out by then. The thought of burying hundreds of them alive isn't a pleasant one.

My dad kicks off his shoes and goes into the kitchen. I can hear him washing his hands at the sink. I should call Amber, I think, to see how her day is going. I felt her tossing and turning last night, probably going over details in her mind. I'll take her out to dinner tonight. But first, I'll make my dad a sandwich, cut up some fruit. Maybe he'd like a beer. I look at the squiggly lines of gray, just slightly lighter than the color around them. I remember when we bought this house, all the plans we had. Some of them happened, some of them changed, and some of them have been forgotten. I wonder what my mom is doing today, whether she's alone. Then I put my dusty shoes next to his and step into the house.

CHAPTER

21

Hallowicz

Woman Starts Over

Mrs. Hallowicz grazed her knuckles on the doorframe as she left her room. She was carrying the box, so she couldn't look down to see what she'd done to her hand. "Goddamn," she said, sucking air through her teeth.

In the kitchen, she put the box onto the table and went over to turn the kettle on. Then she went back to her bedroom and found her shoes and sweater. It was April already but still chilly most mornings, at least to her old bones. It was getting harder to get warm, to keep warm. She was afraid to see what her heating bill would look like this month.

The tea kettle began to whistle as she finished tying her shoes. When she was in New Mexico at Christmastime, Kathy had shown her shoes with two Velcro strips, but Mrs. Hallowicz said she'd never seen anything so ugly in all her days. Her daughter-in-law had seemed surprised, but then she laughed and said Mrs. Hallowicz was right.

She dumped instant coffee granules into a cup of hot water. She wouldn't look inside the box. "Already did that," she said aloud. The box itself was a large shoebox that once held a pair of Wilson's work boots. That alone was hard enough to think about. He was always such a good provider, she thought, such a support. She had spent so many years awash in her own problems, but there'd be no going back to appreciate him more now.

No, she'd spent enough time with the items in the box, enough to have each one set to memory. She had cried and missed and cursed. The photos, the items he made with his own little hands, the blue ribbon from preschool. "Enough," Mrs. Hallowicz said again.

She dug around in a drawer until she found some wide packaging tape and a black marker. Back out to the living room to grab her address book and then, carefully, she copied the name and address onto the front of the box. It took her another trip to the spare bedroom to find a pair of scissors. She had wrapped a few Christmas presents in there before her trip—scarves for Amanda and Joshua, a new shirt for Steven after she asked Rob what size he wore. Things she could easily fit in her old suitcase. She had completely exhausted herself *that* day, finding and retrieving the suitcase from the attic.

In the garage, she nestled the box onto the passenger seat and pushed the button to open the door. Slowly, she backed down the driveway. When she passed the Gleeson's house, Mr. Gleeson was outside, looking at something on the porch. He looked up and gave a weak wave as she passed. Mrs. Hallowicz tried to remember the last time she'd seen him and also tried to remember his first name (was it Dave? Doug?), then she thought about his daughter Sandy Gleeson and her chubby knees.

The drive only took about ten minutes. Back when Wilson had the roofing business, they kept a post office box for business correspondence, and Mrs. Hallowicz had become very familiar with the people working there. That was years ago, of course. She couldn't remember the last time she'd been on a first name basis with anyone.

She stood in line until someone told her she needed to get a paper number from the orange dispenser near the door. She pulled thirty-seven just as someone called out thirty-two. A young man jumped up and offered her one of the few benches in the lobby. She thanked him and decided to remind herself of it whenever she started to feel like young people were a lost cause.

When her number was called, she carried the box to the counter. It wasn't particularly large, but it was heavy. All of the keepsakes from her Stevie's four years on earth, and three 8mm reels, which she hadn't had the heart to watch. She could picture him in her mind's eye; she could recollect his sensory details if she opened that inner door. She wasn't sure what could be done with the old films, but Robbie would know. Rob, she corrected herself.

"Have you filled out one of these?" the man behind the counter asked. He was balding and stooped, leaning forward on a stool. In his hand, some sort of paper.

"No," she said.

"Did you want to insure the items?"

"What does that cost?"

He explained the fee and how long it would take for the box to reach New Mexico. When he saw that it was difficult for her to read the form, he filled it out for her.

"Is this Steven?" he asked, trying to read what she'd written in marker with her shaky grasp.

"Yes," she said. "My grandson. He's thirteen."

He kept writing, looking up once in a while. "Have you been there?" he asked. "New Mexico?"

She cleared her throat. "At Christmas last year. My son bought my ticket."

"How nice," he said. "Was it hot?"

"It was Christmas," she said. "It's not like that. There was frost on the ground in the morning."

"Hm," he said.

Mrs. Hallowicz watched as he got up and put the box with a stack of others behind him on the floor. So many boxes, so many different shapes and sizes, and hers right there on the top, ready for its journey. She took her purse and headed for the door, feeling burdened and lightened all at once.

A Legacy

The first thing Rob noticed was the flowers. Vibrant, colorful rows of them. Purple, white, pink, some sprays of yellow closer to the door. He knew that she had hired a gardener a few years back, but he wondered now if she'd still been doing some of the work. He should have asked. He'd have to find out about the gardener. That went on a mental list.

There were several papers stuck into the crevice of the door; some had fallen onto the dusty porch. Leaning over, he collected everything. He huffed a bit when he stood up. Kathy was right; he really needed to think about getting in shape.

The door creaked open after he turned the key. It was cold and still inside. Dust flurried in clouds when he pulled back the curtains in the front room. He went to the kitchen and threw the papers into the trash can under the sink. Through the window he could see the fence dividing their house from the neighbors, the places the wood had softened and darkened at the bottom. When he leaned forward, he could just make out the pen he and his father had made for the turtle. He should have offered to take it down for her.

The house was really cold, even though it was September and plenty warm outside. He decided to make a cup of something hot. Then he'd walk through and see what he was dealing with, make some lists. When they came out for the funeral, he'd sent Joshua over, just to clear out the perishables, empty the trash, and make sure the door was locked. They only had a few days then, so he knew the house would be sitting until he could attend to it. When an elderly person dies, it never comes as a great surprise and yet, Rob wasn't expecting it. She had just been out for Christmas, and thank God for that. All the kids had been able to come—Steven, of course, but even Amanda, who'd been living in Santa Fe, and Joshua, who flew in from Dallas. He was glad they had a chance to spend time with his mother, and things were uncharacteristically peaceful. She made few sarcastic remarks and was very pleasant to Kathy. And she didn't seem frail at all. Kathy took her to the mall, and she went to Steven's soccer tournament with them. It was as if they had moved beyond a point on the timeline of their lives, some sort of break where the past was out of view.

He started opening drawers, looking for the tea kettle, for coffee or tea. One cupboard was empty, then another. After the fourth, his heart began to race. He hurried around the kitchen, opening every drawer and cupboard, until he finally found something. In the one nearest the refrigerator, there was one fork, one knife, one large plate and one small, one drinking glass and one mug. In the sink, there was a bowl and a spoon, placed neatly next to each other.

Then he noticed. There was nothing on the walls—no pictures, no clock, no calendar pinned next to the door. He went to the living room. Everything gone except the furniture. No photo frames on the mantle, no coasters or magazines on the end table, no knick-knacks. In the hall, the linen closet held one towel and one set of sheets. The bedroom closets were empty, just a few items in his mother's. It was like she'd been living a monk's existence and if he'd bothered to come out here (when was the last time he'd been here?), maybe he would have known. But where was everything?

He stood in his old bedroom, which she had used as a guest room for many years. There was the desk he used through high school, and the same double bed. He remembered now the last time he visited. He had some business in San Diego, so he drove up for a weekend. Steven was a baby then. Could it have been that long?

Suddenly, he turned and rushed down the hall. The door to the garage had a deadbolt that stuck a bit when he turned it. He stepped down and flipped the light on.

She had moved her car to the very left of the garage and parked it so that the door, when closed, was inches from the back bumper. This left much more room for the boxes, many, many boxes, all stacked and lined up against two walls. He walked down the line, reading the labels she had written with a black marker on the front of each box. Dishes (for Goodwill), Books (library or used book store), Clothing (for Goodwill), Pictures (to keep), Personal Items (to look through). She had done everything already. She had packed up her entire house, her entire life, so that he wouldn't have to do it.

Rob stood in the garage and cried and in a little while, he went inside to call Kathy.

Girl Seeks God

Amanda found the cemetery without trouble. Between a high school and a shopping center, close to the freeway, her father told her. There was a mostly empty parking lot next to the straightforward, immense landscape of grass and tombstones. She got out and started to walk. Because it was winter, the grass was marbled with yellow sections and the trees were mostly barren. Wind whipped across the land, causing her to tighten her scarf and shove her hands into her pockets.

Mostly there were flat grave markers, all dark in color, all engraved with the standard information: name, date of birth, date of death. Many had faded or become encrusted with dirt; many were difficult to read. But there were a good number of tombstones, too. When she reached the asphalt road that split the yard into two halves, she passed a tall, cross-shaped stone on the other side. Almost Celtic in appearance, it had a strange figure carved into it. Her father had told her about that, so she started to count the rows back from it.

She hadn't been to California for many, many years. Despite the wintery conditions at the cemetery, during most of her trip she'd been amazed at the colors and greenness. Santa Fe was very much a place of dry earth tones—browns, oranges and during the spectacular sunsets, purple. She had known the first time she went there she would stay. Many great decisions in her life had been made spontaneously. This trip, for example. She had two weeks off from the public defender's office where she worked, and she'd chosen the dates months ago. But only the day before yesterday, she decided to pack up her car and head west. She spent the morning driving around Bellflower, where her dad had grown up and her grandmother had lived, and now she was paying her respects.

She reached the sixth row back from the cross and she started to scan, left to right. Hernandez, Planchett, Smith. Another Smith, and another. She looked back to make sure she counted correctly and then there it was: a joint plaque. Wilson Grant Hallowicz and Elizabeth Mary Hallowicz. And next to that, a smaller memorial for Steven Andrew Hallowicz. Such grand names, she thought. Her memories of her grandmother were few. Sitting on her porch having popsicles, the dusty back yard with the turtle pen, the visit during Christmas right before she died.

Amanda had never been one to follow directions and from the frustrated stories her father told over the years, she'd developed the notion she had inherited the trait from her grandmother. She wished she had made more of an effort to get to know her, but she wouldn't regret it. There had been much growing up to do. Her father had probably hoped for bigger things than a secretarial job, but she was happy with her apartment and her life. She loved Santa Fe, and she had great friends.

She kneeled on the ground and wiped the dust and grass from the marker. It was peaceful, and the sun warmed her back. And when the earth started shaking, it took her a moment to gather her thoughts, to realize what was happening. She fell onto her back and grabbed two fistfuls of grass, while the earth lurched and rolled beneath her. Too quickly it was over, but she stayed on the ground, watching the wisps of clouds as they merged and dissipated, looking for something tangible. And when she finally sat up, she was smiling.

About the Author

Mary Vensel White is the author of *The Qualities of Wood, Bellflower, Starling,* and *Things to See in Arizona.* She's also an editor, a publisher, and an English and writing professor. She lives in southern California.

Read more at www.maryvenselwhite.com

Made in the USA
Columbia, SC
09 February 2024

31143015R00143